THE BOOK OF
SARIEL

KEITH ROMMEL

HELLBENDER BOOKS

an imprint of Sunbury Press, Inc.
Mechanicsburg, PA USA

an imprint of Sunbury Press, Inc.
Mechanicsburg, PA USA

For information about special discounts for bulk purchases, please contact Sunbury Press Orders Dept. at (855) 338-8359 or orders@sunburypress.com.

To request one of our authors for speaking engagements or book signings, please contact Sunbury Press Publicity Dept. at publicity@sunburypress.com.

ISBN: 978-1-62006-809-0 (Trade paperback)

Library of Congress Control Number: 2019940156

FIRST HELLBENDER BOOKS EDITION: April 2019

Product of the United States of America
0 1 1 2 3 5 8 13 21 34 55

Set in Bookman Old Style
Designed by Crystal Devine
Cover by Lawrence Knorr
Edited by Jennifer Cappello

Continue the Enlightenment!

It is strongly recommended that you read all the volumes in the series before committing to *The Book of Sariel*. Reading order:

The Cursed Man

The Lurking Man

The Sinful Man

The Silent Woman

Among the People

Sariêl

The fifth Angel of Apollyon.

The Angel of Death.

The eternal sufferer.

CHAPTER 1

A DEAL

"He killed one of our own," Asmodeus said to the old man, who sat on top of a crocodile. The man had a hawk attached to his fist, and the crocodile was controlled by a simple rope around its neck.

"And what business is it of mine?" the demon known as Agares said. The croc snapped at Asmodeus, who had ventured too close to Agares—or maybe it was the shoes Asmodeus wore.

"If he's killed one, he can kill more. Don't you wish to preserve our kind? Every life matters. There is strength in numbers, and if he depletes our existence one by one, what chances will we have when the time comes?"

"Your point is taken and well received. Remember, he is Death after all. An almost unstoppable force. Who did he kill and why?"

"Orthon. He had lived within a woman since she was a girl. He turned her into something special. As she began the dying process, Sariel took her. He took her before she left her body, and he dragged Orthon to the other side with her. I could feel his fear because he was trapped and had no way back unless Sariel let him go."

"I wonder why he wouldn't let him go."

1

"A play of strength is the only thing I can come up with."

"So, Orthon went deadside. You know that he has no business being there."

"With all due respect, I think you misunderstand what I'm telling you. Sariel dragged him there while he was in a body very much alive. He wouldn't allow him to leave because he was trying to hide what he was doing and possibly to teach all of us a lesson. I say again, imagine if he were to come for us all? Not at once, but as individuals. Imagine the destruction . . . he could lay waste here."

Agares thought. "Yes, that could be a problem."

"I felt Orthon's fear come to a crescendo just before his life was terminated. I felt his pain, too. Sariel is dangerous and needs to be dealt with, and I am the one capable enough to deal with him."

"Agreed that you are." Agares thought some more. His age gave him the wisdom of an old scholar. "I say again, he is Death. He cannot die, and your attempts to make him pay for what he did to Orthon may be futile."

"No, he cannot die . . . but he can bleed. He can hurt."

"Hmm."

"This is why I have come to you, Agares. It is my responsibility to exact revenge on him for what he has done."

"Ahh, yes, the Prince of Revenge: Asmodeus," Agares said. "Careful with whom you tinker. You can be so reckless in your thirst. I've heard about some of your betrothments and how they've stirred unrest. You need to be careful with this one."

"I have learned a great deal since then," Asmodeus said. "I'm not walking into this blindly. No one will know of your part in this, and I have drummed up a plan so precise he will have no time to react until it is already finished."

"I haven't agreed to anything, my neatly dressed Prince of Revenge, because unlike you, I don't wish to draw his attention."

The old man brought the hawk close to his mouth and whispered something to it. It squawked and flew away.

Agares was careful in his position. He had legions of demons under his command and wielded plenty of power to do what Asmodeus wished to achieve. But was his inclusion worth the risk?

Asmodeus was in his territory, uninvited and hoping for two favors from someone he had never met before.

"Yes, revenge is what I seek for what he's done," Asmodeus said. "I don't worry for my safety. I am cunning and eager to make him pay for his trespasses against us, and I am not ill-equipped. You can trust me on this."

Agares laughed. "Trust you?" He turned serious. "I don't even know you, and I know to never trust a demon. I remind you again that you cannot kill Death. Do you remember me telling you this just moments ago?"

"Yes, of course I remember."

"Death *is*, and he's the only one in charge of who lives and who dies. He is eternal and all powerful."

"Not anymore."

Agares raised a thick, long-haired eyebrow.

"I guess it doesn't seem out of line that most don't know," Asmodeus said. "Sariel's not as powerful as he once was. He's given up his post, lost within his own misery, confused and on a mad hunt for something. He's become pitiful, and he's assigned a human in his stead . . . bargained with her so he could venture out. He's vulnerable while he's forfeited some of his power."

"So, what is it you want from me?"

"Two quakes. Small. Just large enough to free Apollyon from his holding cell. He will create the distraction I need."

Clearly, Agares' reputation preceded him. "And how do you suppose to control Apollyon?" he asked.

"I will make him a deal. One he cannot refuse. I cannot go through with my plan without both your inclusion and assistance."

"And what do I get in return?"

"My gratitude. You have all you need, and nothing I offer would be acceptable. And although I am cunning and dishonest, I am not a stupid demon. Simply put, I wouldn't want to insult you."

"Do you say that to soften me?"

"I say that because it is a truth. I recognize who you are and what you are capable of. That is why I'm here and vulnerable to your judgment. Will you help me?"

4

"Maybe," Agares said. The hawk returned with old parchment in his beak. He flew to Asmodeus and hovered, wings swooshing in the air.

"Take the paper," Agares instructed.

Asmodeus took the paper and Agares continued, "Slice your skin. Sign the contract in your blood."

Asmodeus did so without reading what he signed and held it out for the hawk to take. It flew to Agares, and he took the paper, smiled, and waved it gently to dry the blood.

"What do you think, my pets? Do we have a deal?" Agares said and patted the crocodile's head. The hawk squawked, and the croc hissed. A deal had been sealed.

"It seems they like what you ask. Chaos can be good. What will you do with Apollyon once you have finished with him? I'm concerned about him running around. We don't want any attention brought to us, and whatever scheme you have concocted needs to be swift and have a failsafe."

"He will return to where he came from. All I need you to do is close the hole when he's returned to his pit. We both know he must remain there until he's called upon."

"How will I know he has returned?"

Asmodeus pointed at the hawk. "I was hoping you could send him out so he can report back to you. Give you the go-ahead to seal the ground and encase Apollyon once again."

"You ask a lot of me."

"I know I do, but you rule natural disasters upon the earthly plane. You are one of the most powerful, formidable demons I have ever had the pleasure of standing in front of."

Agares liked that. His smile said so.

"I'll do as you ask. Confuse Death if you can, wound him, and make him hurt, I don't care. At best it will bring chaos, and all the lost souls will rain down for us to feast upon."

"I thank you for your cooperation."

Agares allowed his smile to fade. He pulled on the rope, and the crocodile turned him away. "Your quake will come and split the ground soon. I suggest you go and make your deal with Apollyon. Go now. If you are ever called upon, I would expect you to return the favor. He waved the paper. Remember, I have you in my debt."

Asmodeus bowed. "Of course."

He departed in silence, his smile outdoing Agares', because to exact revenge one must be slick. He had no intention of being in service to anyone. Soon, it would be time to bring Sariel to his knees.

CHAPTER 2

SARIEL

The tall, ragged, pale man with a heavy heart pushed his way through the thick, nearly impassable foliage. He used the moonlight as a guide as his long, sharp fingernails worked back and forth to hack away at the branches that grabbed at his robe and skin. He stomped down thick vegetation with raw, bloody feet and pushed on with a grunt.

His body had grown so old and frail, and yet his determination had become unrelenting.

Far off in the distance, he could hear the howl of humanity in distress. Another death; another soul. They came in droves.

Broken.

Unrepentant.

Contagious.

One after the other.

The cry for help—from a sinful man who had come to face the resentment of those who had been cast aside because of his flawed humanity—was filled with tangible fear. The sins of the man were manifested and abandoned here in the Valley, left to wait until death came. And when Death had come for him, the man was set loose in the Valley. Then, the manifestations of his sins began their hunt.

The howls were a part of the chase; so primal and guttural that the skin reacted with horripilation.

He listened some more. It was all around him. Organized panic.

Fear.

Anger.

Run.

Catch him.

Not yet.

Run faster.

Judgment.

Suffering.

Far off and away from where the pale man was, because there wasn't a cabin nearby, the chase continued. But that mattered little now because the pale man was in pursuit of his own reward: a fissure. Slender and tall, like him, hidden by moss and growth—a way in through the back of a winding catacomb without being noticed. He had made this secreted entrance at the dawn of man, sliced into the side of a sandstone, siltstone, and shale wall, deep inside the basin.

Another howl. Louder this time; so loud that it made him turn and look. The sinful man was off his path and drawing near. The things that chased him would shepherd him to where he needed to be in order for the final pursuit to begin. This chase was what the sins longed for: The first taste of what was to be forevermore. They would force the sinful man into a constant state of atonement, to make their creator pay for his trespasses against them—the trespass of having created them in the first place.

The sounds of this chase were nothing new to the pale man and caused him no alarm, the nearness of it all merely a minor distraction from his own search. So, he returned to his task and sank into his thoughts. He had waited a long time to find the right person. Someone who yearned for him and yet feared him.

"Because I," he wheezed, "I am the one thing that has always kept everyone equal. In the end, it is me who decides. Me who they fear. Me who they equally longed for and loathed."

Chance circumstances and the poor choices of others had given him his opportunity, and he unflinchingly took it. Unrehearsed, he negotiated with Cailean to take his place, fully expecting the situation to not work in his favor. But, to his surprise and delight, it would now be she who ushered the dead in his absence.

The pale man briefly listened to the distant, echoing howls. The ongoing chase meant Cailean was doing what she was supposed to: sending souls to their rightful places after death.

"This is good," he confirmed aloud. As he pushed on, branches bent and broke in his wake.

The weight that had been lifted off his shoulders the moment she said yes was so profound that it had brought tears to his eyes. Tears he once had for the people.

"No more," he'd said and meant it.

He had once been a slave but was now freed from his captor; his detainer, the essence of humanity.

The moment he excused himself from his duties was a moment of elation he hadn't felt in eons. It consumed him from head to toe. The hope for this feeling was something he had long ago abandoned, given up on, and then forgotten about. But now that he had it, he felt misplaced, vulnerable, and even a little foolish. The feeling of satisfaction collided with his misery—an emotion he had been drowning in for countless years. An emotion, it seemed, he wouldn't be able to completely leave behind.

Once the human Cailean had died and taken the mantle, the first thing the pale man did was come to the Valley of Death. The flatlands, where he'd normally operated, were now under Cailean's control. And here, in the Valley, was the only other place he wanted to go. But there were other places he *could* go . . .

"No," he said, certain he was on the right path. "Those are places I will never visit without just cause."

A curiosity, overwhelming and unexplainable, had come over him at the moment of transfer, and he came here to discover it. He couldn't label or define this *something* right now, but it compelled him onward. Pulled him through the thicket. Told him to ignore the pain in his old bones and seek it out.

"What is it that drives me to this place?" he mused. "To seek something I know nothing about?" The thought had turned compulsive—recurring and relentless, almost to the point of becoming annoying. To imagine he was being driven by desperation was a paradox. He'd seen people driven by this piti-ful emotion, and it confounded him. Yet, here he was, behaving in a way he couldn't understand.

"What is it?" he wondered aloud again.

His curiosity was matched only by his drive to escape his duties of ushering the dead. With that fierce desire he pressed on, knowing that what he sought was near. It resided beyond the entryway, somewhere deep in the cavern ahead.

"A book," he said. The thought popped into his busy mind. "A book about myself. Written . . ."

His thoughts trailed off, unable to remain fo-cused. A book. Where had that come from? He didn't know, and yet here he was, looking for it. At least now he knew what drove him.

It wouldn't be easy to find, but it would be there, somewhere. Waiting. All these years. Meant to be placed on a shelf and forgotten about. But some-thing had told him a secret. Somehow, the clues to the puzzle unfolded themselves as he continued on his mission.

That thought made him push harder. He plunged through the tangled brush with renewed energy and focus.

Find it.

Open it.

Read it.

Understand it.

The forest had grown so much since he had last used this entrance that he thought he might've gotten turned around somehow. To imagine that

Death, the one to destroy and take away, could create such a lush and thriving environment was yet another paradox.

He shivered and looked up at the moon.

"How could this be? I am the embodiment of cold, and I fear nothing except the power of my own touch!"

He studied his position and tried to rest his mind for a moment from the things that troubled him in this parallel world. Certain he was headed in the right direction and would be on a collision course with the fissure, he continued.

"It has been far too long since I came here. It is pitiful to acknowledge that I have forgotten who I am."

He reached out, took hold of a hefty tree limb, and broke it with his bare hands.

"Damn people."

It had been dozens of human lifetimes since he last saw Twyla. The way she expressed her worry for him the last time he departed had stayed with him on a subconscious level and now returned full-force. It shamed him. Why hadn't he returned sooner? The ominous thing he had said to Twyla before he withdrew was most likely a source of incessant nagging inside her, as she was left to wonder about it for all this time.

He needed to see her but needed to satisfy his own curiosity first. The drive inside made that decision for him.

"If I am right . . . all of this for a book?"

At last, he stopped and faced the wall of rock. It was there, behind a curtain of vines. He reached out his pale, age-speckled hand and gently parted the leaves attached to the heavy cordage. There was the fissure. He slid into it, releasing the vines, which swung back into place and covered the secret entrance, his plowed path seemingly a dead end.

The flicker of firelight from torches that hung on the walls of the hallowed hallway always burned. The imps made sure of that—one of their many deeds as servants to the Angels of Death.

"Death," Sariel grumbled. "I loathe that name. What is death but more life? More suffering? For some . . ."

His words echoed, carrying the distaste he had for the title he had been given so long ago but was unable to shake until this day.

"I am rid of you, and yet I cannot get you off my mind."

As desperate as a man trying to exit his cancer-ridden body, Sariel had tried to abolish himself of the name "Death"—and yet, he looked for it, even though he had only just released himself from its grasp.

"Do you miss me that much?" He sighed. "Or is it I who misses you?"

He looked both left and right and saw the carved-out, incomplete arched hallway that faded into darkness either way. This portion of the tunnel system was still unused. But, as the population grew, so would these halls and the need to fill them with bookcases and finished floors, brighter sconces and more imps.

The smell of death came over him in a wave, and he turned away. No matter how fast he turned or where he moved, the smell followed and assaulted his senses. Then, he realized the stink came from him.

He yanked on his frayed black robe, tried to cut it away like he'd done to the tree limbs outside, but no matter how hard he tried to remove the garment, the material held. It seemed to fight back against his attack. Eventually, he ceased to struggle, tired and out of breath. The garment swayed at his feet.

He whimpered at the possibility that this might be a sign that he could never escape who he was no matter what deal he had made with Cailean. That thought pounded his troubled mind relentlessly, as did the idea that he would never be who he really wanted to be: free of his burdens.

"What is happening to me?"

Resting on one knee, he looked at the blood-stained ground around his feet. Strangely, he didn't think of his physical pain but rather the emotional distress of having been the ambassador of death for so long and the conflict that had begun to rage in his head. It had become a small war of indecision and what-ifs.

"The horror that I am going insane consumes me!"

His hands shook, and his body rattled.

"What has seeing all of the dead, hearing their screams, pleas, and accusations done to me?" The question fell into the blood at his feet and slowly seeped into the dirt. "Will I ever escape it?"

His voice was pitiful and weak, breaking under doubt. His focus shifted back to the cloak and the idea that being unable to shed his clothing was a sign that his plan might have failed. There were far greater forces than he, and he hoped his gamble didn't draw their attention.

A tear fell from his eye, rolled down his face, and dripped off his rounded chin and onto the ground.

The tempest within eased for a moment. It felt good to cry. It had been so long and way overdue. He let the tears flow; his thin shoulders bounced up and down in his delicate sob.

"I loathe you, too," he said and pounded his chest. "How could I not? I abhor the things I've had to see. The things I have been called and needed to do. All in the name of humanity. The broken creatures that carried ire even into death. Unto Death. I rid myself of thee!"

The exchange with Cailean had happened only moments ago, thus this impasse he found himself at fixed him in an unfamiliar place. He had served so long, and he believed that once he severed the tie that bound him, the change of becoming an Angel untethered to the role of Death would happen instantly. That he would feel . . . angelic. But everything here moved so much slower, and he needed to remind himself of that; this 'change' might be gradual.

"Loathe what you were, not what you are now—or seek to be."

He left his face wet and pushed himself to his feet. He grabbed a torch off the wall, held it to his garment, and the cloth lashed out on its own, alive and protective of its bearer and itself. It wrapped the torch, snuffed the flame with a mighty squeeze, and then released the burnt remnant.

"What is this?" Sariel asked and slammed the smoldering torch onto the ground. The few remaining embers jumped out like sparks. He looked in both directions of the hallway again. The puddle of blood where he stood had absorbed into the dirt floor.

"This," he said and grabbed the fabric. He studied it, and it remained limp in his hand. "This has never happened before."

He let the cloak fall into place, and he looked in either direction again.

"This way," he said, and went right. If memory served him correctly, that was the quickest way to get to his destination.

"The book. Within those pages must be instructions on how to get this off! I must have written it to myself as a reminder."

His wiry, haggard legs moved him along briskly.

"Cailean," he muttered again and again.

He was not oblivious to the obsession he had for her. After all, she was the woman who had taken over his role as Death. It required him to study her life, for him to live it with her so he knew everything there was to know.

Her sentence was well deserved, but the way he fooled her into believing she had twenty-four hours to make things right after the deal was done was deceit on his part.

The lie was deliberate.

Words meant to sell his proposal.

There was no chance for her to make anything right.

Maybe he didn't have that chance either.

He was becoming like them in his desperation, and as much as he tried to shun the thought, it persisted. He was dishonest with himself and devoid of any real conviction about it. That was, until now.

"Is that how this works? Guilt after the misdeed but no conscience while it's being done?"

His mind couldn't comprehend, and his head began to hurt as much as his decrepit limbs.

"She won't remember what I did, and I don't care if she does anyway. I am free of that life. Calling her horrible, deplorable even, was being too soft." His voice was his lone companion as he moved along. "She was the epitome of humanity broken. The very thing that broke me along the way."

Yet, he found something appealing about her; that was why he was drawn to her in the first place. The allure of her persistence. The way she harbored Orthon, the demon within, and how she suppressed compassion and all love and continued to have the desire to live. To go on when there was nothing left to live for, with only a demon to keep her company.

What now accompanied him?

Sariel hurried.

"Why? Why did people do that? How could she carry on in the face of such odds?

"Yes, she attempted suicide, but no real effort went into taking her life. So, the question begged when you are that broken: What was the use in carrying on?

"For misery's sake," Sariel supposed. "Misery has its place in this world and theirs. I sit in it, try to understand it, but it doesn't allow me in. It just *is*. Taunting. Maybe that is the way it was for her too."

The flawed mechanics of humanity were a plague, an endemic contagion. And the more and more he was left to think about it, the more he couldn't help but acknowledge who he was becoming . . . if he hadn't transformed already.

"But that's what humans do to themselves and others. They infect," Sariel said, his voice a dull echo, poor company. "They don't care until it is too late. So many just don't care at all, and I was called upon to try and fix the unfixable. So, I created the Valley . . . for God is not here. There are only the sinful and their sins.

"It was me they ended up hating and blaming, so how could I not inevitably hate and blame them back? How long until one grows tired of endless accusations and ghastly labels that are clearly misplaced?"

Soon, the dirt floor and walls became brick, the arches finished. Here, the sconces burned brightly. The soot stains behind the flames were a welcome sight; these torches burned the brightest and had been burning the longest. Not for his eyes, rather, but for the imps to see; darkness held no dominion over him.

Sariel had made it to the Akashic Halls. Books bound in leather, old and new, occupied the shelves. Cataloged in a very specific order, alphabetical and by arrival date, he supposed, these volumes were organized and handled by the imps—creatures he had little interest in and discarded after they'd served their purpose.

They would usher the books into the cabins, and after a person was judged, they moved the books to a holding chamber that spiraled deep into the earth, centered beneath the Akashic Halls. It was a place they called the Void. Things were done but yet unfinished, leaving behind a gaping hole—hence the name.

"I surround myself in oddities."

That he had written these books showed his commitment. He'd meant well for so long, never once wavering in his thoughts until recently. The initial reasons for his change of heart were unknown to him, of course, with the exception that he had determined that humanity had brought him to this: a breaking point.

But, maybe there were more answers in this special book he sought. It had to be something clearer than his clouded feelings of resentment, lack of self-worth, and a sense of duty left behind.

At a break in a hallway, he changed directions, heading down a corridor that curved like a snake.

An imp came into view. Busy in its task, it fluttered over to a bookshelf, scanning the selections with its beady black eyes encased in fire-red skin and a bone-like mask face. It moved to another section then caught a glimpse of Sariel and came to him quickly.

It hovered, and Sariel stopped walking. The imp, no taller than twelve inches, landed on his shoulder, hugged his neck, took hold of Sariel's long, floppy ear, and whispered into it.

"Twyla misses you so. I've seen her cry. She does that a lot lately, and I don't know why. Trouble occupies her cabin as we speak."

"What sort of trouble?"

"A sinful man. One who is breaking the rules. He's reckless. Out of control. Threatening, even. I wish I could help, but I know I cannot. I have so much work to do."

The imp flew away and returned to his mission of finding some particular book. Sariel was only a few minutes away from where he thought he needed to be when he wrestled with the idea of checking on Twyla or continuing with his quest. He decided that she was tough and could handle herself, and she had Keir as well.

He started again to walk toward the books, then stopped. Hesitation as yet another battle surged within. Why resist it? He resigned with a sigh. His indecision about putting himself before the needs of his long-lost love was yet another indication that humanity had tainted him. He wished he could scrub it off his body and out of his mind.

His soul was scarred and bleeding. Lost, hollow, and alone in its struggle to grasp onto a sense of normalcy—of what was supposed to be his new normal. Sariel turned around. His stiff legs and painful feet cracked and crunched as they carried him toward Twyla's cabin.

CHAPTER 3

TWYLA

Sariel remained in the dark. He watched Keir fetch water out of a basin and run into the main portion of the cabin, yelling.

Broken furniture littered the central room inside the cabin, and a young man ran around in desperation, trying to keep the firelight from dying. Once it went out, Sariel knew that the man would have to go outside to face the things his sins had created. The frantic man tore at his clothes and brandished some sort of stick.

"Now get out, mister," Keir said. The flames in the fireplace sizzled, dimming the interior of the cabin. "You're more trouble than you're worth."

Sariel moved closer. He knew there were tough cases like this one, but that Twyla and her ward could handle themselves. However, since he was here, he could intervene . . . For now, he stood in the shadows to remain undetected.

The sinful man raised a glowing torch, apparently made from some cloth wrapped around a chair leg, which he'd dipped into the fire before Keir extinguished it completely. He ran out of the cabin, the torch spewing black soot that dissipated into the night.

Twyla glared at Keir. "Look at what he's done!"

"I'm afraid it seems as though they're getting worse," Keir said. By his looks, one would think Keir was just a boy. In truth, he was thousands of years old.

Sariel stepped into the room and removed his hood.

"Twyla."

Twyla stopped and stared at him. Her old eyes didn't blink; it appeared as though his presence didn't register. Her wrinkled face showed her confusion.

"I have come," he said and took a step forward.

Her jaw dangled, eyes transfixed.

"When I arrived in the Valley, I was told you were having trouble. I stood in silence and watched, just now, knowing you and Keir could handle yourselves. But I came here, just in case you might need me."

Finally, those words, his gravelly voice: It clicked.

"Sariel!" Twyla said and hobbled to him. She took his hands into her own gnarly hands and looked deep into his white, marble-like eyes. "You came back!"

"Yes, I've come. I told you I had something big planned, and I finally did it."

"That was so long ago I had almost given up."

"I was unsure . . . careful . . . thought it through and needed to be patient . . . precise. Today, I finally acted."

"What is it?" Twyla said as she leaned into Sariel like a young girl melting at the sight of her first love returned home from a long-fought war. "Tell me what it is you have done."

Sariel looked at Keir. The boy worked at cleaning up the mess the sinful man had left behind, but Sariel knew that children liked to eavesdrop.

"Not here," he said and squeezed her hands reassuringly.

"Then where?"

"The room behind . . . the Akashic Halls," he said and turned. He gave her hand a gentle tug, and together they exited the cabin and entered the back room from which he'd emerged to watch the chaos.

The room they stood in now was a judgment room that connected directly to the Akashic Halls. Twyla had used it often to show the truth to sinners—a truth impossible to ignore once presented.

"Wait," Sariel said.

"What is it?"

Sariel let her hand go, walked to middle of the mostly empty room, and sat on the tree stump in its center, his back to her. A massive blank wall stood in front of him, and a tree reached the ceiling in the corner.

"I need to see," he said.

"That mirror isn't intended for us to use for ourselves. We are different."

"Are we?" Sariel's sagging face managed little expression. "But yet you use it all the time to prove a point, don't you?" He raised a brow. "To prove what's inside? I don't think we are that different."

Twyla shivered at his words and what he was looking to have her do. "Yes, of course. You designed it. You know what it does."

"So, then; let us see. Shall we?"

Her silent expression of protest shifted as her eyes grew sad inside her wrinkly mask.

"Please, Twyla, light the candles for me."

"What are you looking for, Sariel?"

"Truths. I'm prepared to face what I see. I have my suspicions, as I'm sure you do. You can sense these things. Somehow, I suspect you know some of the reasons why I have come."

"I don't—"

"Please," Sariel said and raised a hand. "No need to defend my allegations. All I need to know right now is what my time around humans has done to me."

"That doesn't matter," she protested. "You don't need a mirror to tell you that. Look inside yourself and tell me how you feel."

"Lost," Sariel said without hesitation. "Forsaken. Betrayed. Confused." He rested his elbows on his knees and seemed to talk to the ground between his feet. "Shall I go on?"

She stared at him wordlessly.

"Now, please, light the candles and let's have a look," he said and sat upright.

Twyla trudged to the tree in the corner. Sariel studied the twisted trunk and its crooked branches, reminding him of his own body. Twyla went about lighting the candles on the branches. One by one, they cast a little more light and revealed a heartbreaking truth.

Sariel shifted his attention from the branches to Twyla. Old feelings came flooding back, and he wanted to tell her so. But, before he could speak of his emotions, the mirror wall came to life. Distracted, he peered into it, watched the light grow brighter still. What stared back at him was abominable.

"Come behind me, my love," he said. "Let's take a look together."

Twyla stood behind him and draped a hand over his bony shoulder, but she didn't look up.

"Why won't you look? Am I that hideous?"

"No. I'm afraid of what you're trying to show me."

"Just the truth, Twyla. That is what I'm after. Please, for my sake, look at us."

Twyla looked up. She tried to hide her surprise, but how could she?

He thought he saw a slight flinch. He looked exactly the way he felt, and he would never forget her reaction to it. This moment profoundly cemented him into his feelings.

"I know," he said and petted the back of her hand. "I don't blame you."

Sariel stared at the reflected image of a young, beautiful woman where Twyla stood. Her majestic white wings flared out, flapped assuredly to rid themselves of the stiffness of having been tucked away for so long and then quickly pulled back in.

"You see how beautiful you are? Don't hide that." He turned to face her. "But that isn't the only reason I fell in love with you. It is because of what this mirror reveals—the beauty that is inside of you is untouchable. Even for the wayward who look at you with lies and ill intent."

Sariel turned once more toward the mirror and studied himself. Ragged black robe; pale, drawn face; long, stretched ears; sad eyes; gnarled hands and skinny legs hidden beneath the drape of the protective robe. Vile both inside and out.

"Look at me." He sat still and stared. "I've allowed them to corrupt me. I realized that during my journey here. That's what I want to convince myself of, anyway. I have known what resides in you just as I know I have become no better than them."

Twyla scowled. "How could you say that after all the good you've done?"

Sariel pointed at his mirror image. "Because I have proof, and it stares us right in the face. It's undeniable!"

"You don't need to look at that," Twyla said and hurried to extinguish the light. "I know who you are and what's inside of you. You may be confused right now, uncertain about feelings you're unfamiliar with. You need to give yourself time. Reflect and adjust."

"I'm not so sure that will help me."

He struggled to stand. His old, tired legs wobbled, popped, and crunched. Twyla dashed to help him.

"Don't! I've got it!"

Twyla backed away. His tone was harsh enough to freeze her, mid-assistance.

He watched her face. She seemed shocked by the emphasis he had used. That bite of anger was misdirected and divisive and never had he been anything but pleasant. That is, until recently.

"I'm sorry, but can't you see?" he said, finding comfort in pulling the hood over his head. The blackness was just so familiar, so safe. A place to hide from judging eyes. "Please understand that it is not you," he said. "You are the most precious thing to me, and I would never hurt you. You are the one I've always thought about returning to. The only one I have ever loved. I couldn't wait to look into your eyes again."

Another lie. All he wanted to do right now was search the Akashic Halls. Look for a book. But why? What had changed in him?

"You have come," she said and reached for his ice-cold hand. "You have come, and that is all that matters to me. The rest can be worked out."

"Look at how I've aged," he said, holding up the bumpy knuckles of his hands, twisted and knotty from years of unending toil. The shimmering paleness from being submerged in the darkness for so long radiated from his skin.

Two angels in service of the dead since the creation of man, once they had both been beautiful, but the unforgiving road they traveled had affected them but, each differently.

"Damn," Sariel said. The condition of his body was the least of his worries—his mind was amiss, polluted and disorganized.

Twyla limped, a hunch to her back. Her nightgown was worn to bare threads, and her toes hung over slippers too small for her feet. Her nails clicked on the floor with each step. Her eyes, however, showcased the youth hidden within. Though she appeared to all who entered the Valley as a decrepit, frail old crone, her aging was an artificial ruse; the fallen who crossed over here were undeserving of her true angelic appearance. So, her outward appearance had eroded over the years as a result of the depravity she'd been exposed to. A reflection of who and what she'd been in contact with.

Sariel's aging, however, was genuine, inside and out. The mirror showed that. His hair was gone, his eyes were sad, and his thin, unsteady limbs barely cooperated to carry him along each painful step.

Together, Sariel and Twyla walked for a while in silence. His thoughts raced with a million questions, a million scenarios on what could be . . . but he had said enough, and what was said needed to stay out there for a little while longer, undisturbed. He needed to help her understand.

It wasn't that Twyla could do anything about Sariel's change anyway; but to know that she would try to help him move past this was enough for the time being.

Proof simmered in the way she remained hushed and went where he led her.

"I think something happened to me," he said.

"What do you mean?"

"My tone of voice, the bite it carries. These thoughts that whirl inside my head."

"You're upset."

"I think I'm something more than that. You sense my distress, know it runs deep, and yet you say so little."

"Because I believe in you. You will find your way."

Sariel carried on in silence, and Twyla kept pace.

"I believe in you," she said again.

"I don't know for how long."

"Why do you say these things, Sariel? Why?"

"Because it is the truth."

"You're being vague and evasive. Tell me what is going on."

"The things you do, I can do no longer," he said.

"What do you mean by that? I asked you to stop being vague."

"Look at my body. Is not what you saw in that mirror proof enough?"

"Have you been called home? Is that what you've come to tell me?"

Sariel waved a dismissive hand. "No. I've heard nothing from home since this all started. I'm afraid they've forsaken us. But I've done something. Something you may not like."

"What is it?"

He hesitated. "I've abandoned my post, Twyla."

Twyla stopped, slowly circled Sariel, and stood in front him. She looked up and into the blackness of his hood. He knew she could see within.

"What do you mean you abandoned your post?"

"I've left it. I never plan on going back there. I have this place I'd like us to go to—"

"No," Twyla said and shook her head. "You can't just quit, Sariel. You know this."

"Well . . . I did it. I needed to."

"But why?"

"I—I think I've become attached to things on the other side . . . become curious about their life. Curious about mine. I don't know."

"They live blindly while we have full knowledge."

"No," Sariel said. "That is where you're wrong. We do not have full knowledge."

Twyla looked at him, her eyes a question mark.

"Not to worry. Someone else is there now. Someone who willingly took my place. I offered her a gift of life in exchange for my post, and she took the deal."

Twyla's face contorted with disbelief. It hung there for a while, frozen in wonder, then suddenly morphed into disgust. "What did you see while you were doing this? What you did with her—whatever you saw—that's what changed you. Why would you allow yourself to get so close?"

"I don't know," he said and pushed her hand away. "But this is my domain, and I can do as I please. I've been left here since the Garden was contaminated by the serpent, and I've been given no direction."

"You didn't need direction! You had trust! Look at what you've built. The processes you've put in place! The angels who have followed you here to help you!"

"If they didn't follow they would've been forced. I volunteered, yes, but I wonder if I really did."

"Your thinking, Sariel—it is so perplexing to me. You should not bargain with a human, having experienced the things you have, and expect to come out unscathed."

"I was broken before I went to her."

"But you can't give someone death in exchange for life. What were you thinking?"

"That it was my way out. That I no longer had to serve. So I could come and take you away with me to that special place I mentioned."

Sariel stepped around her and continued.

"You may not see things my way right now, but the feeling that is burning within me has guided me this far," he said. He reached back and took her hand, again encouraging her to come along.

"Guiding you to do what?"

"You'll see." What words could he use when he barely understood himself? He paused, looked into her eyes. "Don't you trust me anymore?"

"What do you want me to say? It's like I don't even know you anymore. What do you intend to do?"

"Hold your judgment. Come, you'll see."

Sariel took to silence again, careful in the words he was to choose. Perhaps his desire to find answers was meant for him alone.

"I'm not going with you," Twyla said as if in response to his thought.

He stopped. It was as if she could read his mind. But that was an impossibility.

For him to think his journey should continue alone was one thing, but to hear her say it was something else entirely. How he wished she'd take back those unsupportive, cold words.

Twyla stopped too and looked back at the path they had traveled: Sariel's bloody footprints leading right up to where they stood.

"This feeling I have," he said. "It's hard to explain. Don't you wish to help me come to terms with it?"

He leveled his gaze to meet hers, reached out to touch her, and she backed away. Of course she would after the things he had said and done. She was the embodiment of nurturing and helpfulness; of course she would recoil from his selfishness because she was repulsed by it.

"I want to share with you," he said.

"I have waited for you for so long. Always have. But for you to come to me like this, telling me these things . . . it's as if you are a stranger to me."

"I intend to find out the truth about myself," he said. "What I am. Put out this fire within. Maybe understand what the people really are. Because as I stand here before you, who I was is no more. You need to grasp that."

Twyla thought for a moment. "There is no great truth to the universe that we don't already know."

"Look at the complexity of the people we judge. What do you really claim to know about them?"

She blinked.

"Me too." Sariel shrugged. "But if you will follow me, you'll see just as I will."

"Why do I feel like I'm losing my best friend? The man who has led me all these years? Taught me honor and obedience."

Sariel didn't answer. He took a step and encouraged her along by intertwining his ancient hands into hers.

"If I were to look my name up in these halls and there was a book, where would we find it?"

"You are on a witch hunt, Sariel. Stop roaming these halls and fix what you have done. Relieve this woman in your post. Do it now, I beg you."

Sariel stopped, faced Twyla, took her other hand, and looked at her. "I can't. Time has kept us apart. Our service to the people has kept us apart. We are together now; standing here for a reason. I want to know what it is and share it with you. This discovery can be great. It can be life changing."

Twyla stared at Sariel, and he watched her expression crumble.

"What is it? Why do you look at me so? I'm trying so hard to include you. To let you inside my heart and my mind, but you defy me."

"You've written all of these books, Sariel. How could you hope to find something you yourself don't know about when it is you who created it?"

With those words a thought hit him, and it took him a moment to come to terms with it.

"Because I don't believe I am the only one who has written books here. Someone else has roamed these halls besides the Angels of Death and the imp servants."

"Like who?"

"I don't know."

"You are wrong. It has always been us and never anyone different."

The two stood together and looked at the great hall. It branched off in every direction, hundreds of thousands of leather-bound books from floor to ceiling, endless rows down each corridor, disappearing into the millions.

"You are on a senseless quest," she said. "But as senseless as it is, you are also creating danger for everyone. Can't you see past your own selfish needs?"

"It will only take us a few moments. Prove me wrong then. Accompany me, and let's see together that there is indeed no book."

"I can't do that."

"Why? If I am wrong, I will remove Cailean from her duties of being Death and I will return, never to do this again. But if I am right—"

"Listen to yourself, Sariel. You are not being logical and I should go. I'm hoping you will trust in me and follow where I go."

CHAPTER 4

THE PIT

A subtle crack split the earth, and suddenly the ground spread. It sounded like a moan, an awakening of something wicked.

Dirt and debris collapsed inward as the gap began to stretch. It reached out with spidery tendrils, widening, forming a growing sinkhole that swallowed the woodsy area of its birth. It ate the trees, the plant life, and animals that tried to scurry out of the way but didn't make it in time. The bedrock grumbled as it yawned open, nothing in its path safe.

After deafening cracks and crunches that rumbled deep underground and shook the earth, the chasm settled and spewed smoke into the air like a gigantic furnace.

Silence befell the forest. No bird called, no four-legged creature sought its next meal or dashed about. Even the bugs that littered the once-busy forest floor went into hiding.

A terrible sound came from the hole.

Inhuman.

Evil.

Angry.

Awakened.

Splintered rock jutted all the way down to the bottom of the deep black pit. There, inside the schism, hunched a creature that had been chained to the wall. The crack in the rock had shifted just so that it snapped the shackles. He was finally without restraints. Disbelieving at first, he unfolded from the fetal position and stood upright. The chains dangled from his wrists, broken, and he tossed them aside. He was free at last, his movement no longer inhibited. Everything around him smoldered, and steam hissed as it blasted from below and sped for the surface.

The creature had yellow eyes, long ago morphed from a majestic blue so he could adapt and see in the dark. He looked around and saw others chained to the walls. None of them were as lucky as he. They were still bound by their chains, stuck, meant to remain, to suffer torment for their trespasses. They were his people, the ones he fell with, and he knew he couldn't break the chains to free them. Their bonds were far too strong, and he was weakened from being dormant for so long. A shaky, pitiful voice called for his help.

"Apollyon, please release us."

"I cannot," he answered. He looked up. It was a struggle to stay upright. "I need to conserve all of my energy for the climb to the surface."

The sky above had darkened, and the rainfall was heavy. Drops touched his hot, fire-red skin and sizzled. "I cannot break the chains that bind you any more than you can help me do whatever it is I've been freed for."

"What are you being sent to do?"

"I don't know. I'm not sure I care either."

"They could be setting you up. Knowing you are weak. Traveling to the surface alone is a risk."

"One I must take."

Another puff of steam rushed past him, but his flesh had hardened over time, like iron made malleable by flame and then plunged into water, sealing its shape. He could no longer feel the heat. The beast had been forged by fire, and he wore the smell of brimstone.

"Apollyon is right. He cannot do a thing for us," another said, chained off in the darkness, on his knees, his head down, his long hair like a curtain to hide his grotesque features. "For whatever reason, this hole has been opened, it has chosen him, and he must do what must be done. If we were meant to help, he alone would not have been freed."

"I am the one that has freed you," a demon said. Little gave away that he was indeed a demon. He was dressed fancily in a top hat, pinstripe suit, and alligator-skin shoes.

"Who are you and how did you get in here?"

"The real question is, what do you have to do to get out of here? Who I am matters little. I have my own agenda, and it allows you to roam the surface world for a little while."

"Free me," one off to the side said. "I will do your bidding."

"No, my choice has been made, and it is a good choice."

"What do you need from me?"

"I know you are the Lord of the Locusts. Set them free upon the world and retrieve something for me. If you agree to my terms, then climb out of this hole, uphold your end of the deal, and your prize will be great. Falter, and I will have you returned to the pit and chained so that you may never get out again."

The man in the suit turned and walked away, disappearing into the puffs of steam.

"What is it I'm supposed to do?" he called out.

Just then, Apollyon gagged, and everyone looked at him.

He heaved again, and his eyes bulged and watered; drool spilled from his mouth. He heaved again and again, each time his mouth stretching wider and the sound of his retching louder. He was unable to hide his concern and looked to his friends for guidance.

Eyes from all around just stared back at him. What could they say?

Then he threw up bile, gagged one last time, and with that, a bevy of locusts poured out of his mouth and rushed topside. One remained behind, crawled upon his shoulder, and took to his ear. Apollyon knew this was the one sent by the finely dressed man who had freed him. The terms and conditions delivered through Apollyon's own power—from the whisper of a locust—something he hadn't loosed upon the world in centuries.

"Ah," Apollyon said, smiling, liking what he heard. "I gladly accept those terms. To allow me such privileges, how could I refuse?"

Although limited in time to get done what was needed, he was set free to roam about, to leave his mark upon the earth like a deep gash into flesh.

The clatter of the thing that had his ear rang in his head. He despised that it told him what to do, as he would rather do what he desired than operate under the command of another. But what a small price to pay to escape this Hell! Even if only for a little while; to reap his reward and fulfill his agreement by returning here.

He grabbed the locust, and in a statement that his control was only conditional, he tossed it to the ground and stomped on it.

The guts strung from the ground to his foot the way gum does to the sole of a shoe. He wiped his feet, rubbed his hands together at the chance he'd been given, and studied the jagged wall. He calculated the path he would take. It would bring him around the circular hole as if climbing up a corkscrew.

Apollyon's thick, calloused hands gripped the bulging, sometimes unsteady rock, and he climbed, his eyes on the surface world. One foot found stability on an outcropping, and then the other. His hand reached up, pulled his body upward as his feet felt for new purchase again, and he repeated the process. He was down much deeper than he thought; his climb would be long and strenuous. With his breathing already labored and his strength wavering, the first order of business when he reached the top would be to get some much-needed nourishment.

"Apollyon, please don't leave us here!" a voice cried out.

"I told you, he must!" another shouted, the volume of his voice knocking debris from the unsteady wall. "Don't you think if he could free us all, he would? We are brothers."

Apollyon looked down upon his chained counterparts, now some forty feet or more below him, partially encapsulated in darkness and swirling steam. The second captive was right. There was nothing he could do, because if he could, they would all be free and setting the world on fire. So, he turned his attention upward. The anticipation of taking a clean breath of fresh air made him push harder, ignoring the fatigue in his atrophied muscles and hastening his ascent to the surface world.

Solid foundation for the feet, then the hands, was the key to working his way up, sidestepping, propelling straight up, and stopping when required. Although he was short of breath and a tremble had consumed his weak body, he continued his climb, defiant every inch of the way.

Finally, his adrenaline kicked in, and with each movement it felt as though his strength was growing, but along with it, so did his hunger.

He repeated the process over and over, speeding the progress, wearing himself down and harnessing his hunger again, and he soon became reckless in his pursuit to reach the top.

Desperate.

He lost his footing and dangled over the deep maw, his fingers slipping. Despite the danger, he remained calm and swung his legs until he found a sturdy rock to place his feet. And there, on that rock, he felt the cool air from above rush into the hole. He could feel it on his skin, the freedom beckoning from up above. He took a moment to close his eyes and embrace it.

It had been so long since he had felt something so wonderful.

"I will be back," he shouted into the pit. "And I will bring you all something great upon my return. Something far beyond your imaginations. Believe in your brother. I do this not just for myself but for all of us."

CHAPTER 5

FRIENDS

"This is where we should live," Collier said. "Look at this shit. Not a human being around for miles to screw anything up."

Will sipped a beer, an amused smile pulling at his lips. They sat on the porch of a rented cabin deep in the middle of nowhere. The mountainous view was breathtaking, the distant valley beyond nestled perfectly in the cusp of tall peaks where fluffy white clouds drifted and covered the trees.

No one around for miles was right; though Collier was the only human being needed to screw something up.

Collier sat forward in his chair, his elbows on his knees. "I appreciate you treating me to this. You take care of me. You're so generous to me it kind of makes me sick. But, seriously. You know how much I appreciate it when you do shit like this."

"I know," Will said. "You over-thank me, and I tell you that you don't have to do that. I'll say it again: You don't need to thank me. We've been friends far too long for that. This is the sort of thing we do for each other."

Will Garavuso and Collier Steadman were the best of friends and had been since childhood. Polar opposites, Will had excelling in academics and the Boy Scouts, sang in the church choir, and was a violin virtuoso by the age of 17. In contrast, Collier was in constant trouble. He skipped school, loved to drink and smoke, and found himself in detention every time he showed up for school. He thought church was a joke, God a trap for the weak-minded, the violin gay, and the Boy Scouts just as gay—all of which he'd proclaimed loudly and often. Courts didn't scare him, and the police were simply horrible people to run away from—which he did whenever those authorities complicated his life.

Collier had tried to influence Will to see things his way, but Will's foundation was firm, and his vision set on his future. Will's father didn't like troublemakers and often forbade the friendship that had turned into a secret bond by the tenth grade.

If they hadn't lived down the block from one another, they probably never would have made such good friends or tolerated the other's differences throughout the years. In fact, more sensibly, they would have made perfect enemies. Instead, they had developed the oddest friendship in the entire school. Collier would even protect Will as if he were a big brother.

But now they were adults, and they had both learned the hardships life can bring. Their respective parents had passed, and the harshness of looking out for themselves had become reality by the time they had reached the age of twenty-five.

Will had made the most of it, now a successful, high-end lawyer, while Collier drifted from job to job, most of the time making just a few dollars above minimum wage. He'd held onto his latest job for more than six months. In his view, that was half of a lifetime and nothing short of a miracle.

Collier held his beer aloft in a toast to his friend. "Yeah well, I'm going to do it anyway," he said. "Thanks is the least you can get for taking care of my lazy ass."

"You work, Collier. You're not lazy."

Collier chugged a beer, let out a long, throaty burp, and laughed at himself.

"You ready for another?" Collier said and dug into the cooler that was positioned between their two chairs. "This conversation is getting way too deep, and it requires a buzz."

Will held up his beer, which was three-quarters full. "I'm good for a while."

"Still on your first one?" Collier shook his head. "Like sucking on that tit, huh?" He cracked open another. "The kids?" he asked, taking a swig.

"Doing great. Two and three years away from attending college," Will said.

Collier cocked his head. "No shit?"

"I know," Will said and paused. He stared around at the landscape and took the setting in, his eyes locked on the bounty of nature. He took a small sip. Will enjoyed the taste of beer but didn't like drinking to the point of feeling sick the next day. Slow and steady. Enjoy what he had. "Do you realize it has been over four years since our last vacation?"

Collier tried to hide his surprise by emptying half of another bottle.

"We're like a damn snowball rolling down one steep-ass hill, aren't we?"

Will smirked. "Great analogy. Got the whole visual and everything. But yeah, it creeps up on you, family and all. Jobs . . . life. That's the stuff we get caught up in. Adding a thin layer at a time till the snowball is a snow boulder."

Collier pulled the bottle away from his mouth and studied the clouds in the valley. They looked like they were darkening, taking the form of a storm. They swirled around, but slowly, non-threateningly. Maybe the storm would pass them by.

"It seems like only yesterday I was skipping class and you were getting straight As. Your voice of reason echoes in my head to this day. I wonder what things would have been like if I would have turned my back on the idiots I kept trying to impress and concentrated on my future."

Will shrugged. "Who knows? Maybe this is the way things are supposed to be."

"Maybe. But having been dealt those cards? It's shitty from this seat."

"I don't know if I've ever told you this, but the job, the money . . . sometimes I don't think it's worth it."

"What do you mean?"

"How long have I had the firm now, twenty years?"

"Has it been that long?"

"Repetition. Unhappiness. My complaining, greedy partners that I have to watch over like a hawk . . . sometimes I see no end in sight. The paycheck gives me things like this. Things to keep me busy. Keep the wife busy. To escape reality with my friend after years and years have gone by and I didn't even realize it. But mostly, it keeps me from taking a moment to see what is really important."

Will mused that jobs had a way of doing that to people—even the ones that appeared to be the most glorious. Grand paychecks, boats, cars, parties, expensive jewelry, and a trophy wife. Maybe it was just some sort of replacement or a distraction for a void. Fill it with things; things that had no meaning, really, so that way you wouldn't have to look at it—or look at what was coming after you, once your time on this earth was through.

"I'm surprised to hear that," Collier said. "I never sensed that from you. The cookouts, parties . . . all the get-togethers."

"Well, I guess it needed to be said then. I mean, look. Here is something important. It helps us breathe. Besides that, it's just beautiful." Will splayed his arms wide, presenting the forest.

Collier laughed. "Yeah, sure, you could have ended up like me with a dead-end, mediocre-paying job—or jobs, for that matter. I'm given horrible benefits where the boss of the company doesn't give one little crap about me. It's so damn easy to tell them to screw off when they don't pay you enough to buy toilet paper so you can wipe your ass."

"I suppose I should count my blessings."

"I suppose you should, Bible boy," Collier said, his response in jest. "It is a far cry from the old days when a company respected you, cared, and paid you what you were worth. Now the workplace has become so bad that you arrive late or make one mistake—" Collier clapped his hands once— "BAM, out the door you go! Not even a kick in the ass or an 'F-you' to take with you on the way out the door. They don't care if you have family or not. Kids. Mortgage. Makes no difference. It's so damn cutthroat. That's why I stay alone and rent a small place. It just makes things easier."

Will shook his head. "I hear about how bad the job market is all the time."

"Clients?"

"Yeah. And some friends."

"Figured as much." Collier finished his beer and took another and held it up. "I'm not even going to bother asking if you want one."

Will paid Collier no mind. He looked out, immersed in the luxury of greenery. "I didn't realize how much I needed this. Work, family . . . it all starts to blend together, doesn't it? Although it's right there in front of you, sometimes you just don't see it. Or better yet, it's easy to forget why you're doing it in the first place. We become blind, numb, and cultured to just *be*."

"I'll drink to that," Collier said, needing no excuse, really. He looked at his friend and noticed for the first time the crow's feet around his eyes. "We're getting old, Will. You're getting wrinkles and shit."

"I was thinking the same thing about you. You're getting really gray. You should dye that. It would probably take about three days off."

"Kiss my ass, would ya?"

"Yeah, yeah."

The clouds rolled in the distance.

"What you were saying is true though. We seem to lose ourselves in all the crap along the way. I try and tell a lot of my bosses that the meaning to life is not to live to work but to work to live. I mean, these guys put in fifty, sixty hours a week without batting an eye. It seems too much to me. Everyone forgets that, and that's how things become so mundane and muddled. Get some paychecks, go shopping, work, eat, sleep, and repeat. Half of them probably don't even get to see their spouses or children. Then, the next thing we know, we take a moment to pick our heads up and half our adult life is gone, parents are dead, and your kids are all grown, and I'm sitting here like holy crap, where did the time go?"

Will nodded. "I almost felt guilty leaving the wife and kids behind, but I know how bad I needed this . . . you too."

"This newest job I have?" Collier said and then gave a long pause. He sipped the beer as his eyes pulled inward with his thoughts. "Plainly put, the boss is an asshole. I can't stand when you have someone over you, you know, like a manager, that you can do the job so much better than. So many times I just wanted to quit. It seems so easy and yet it is so impossible."

"That impossibility is called responsibility," Will said.

"No, it's called a shitty economy."

Will heard a noise in the forest to his left and looked toward the sound. Collier didn't seem to notice Will's curiosity.

"The same desk, sitting behind it day after day, staring at the same smudges on the wall. I put a fingerprint on my wall like six months ago and the damn thing is still there. It's kind of like me spray painting my name on the side of the school when I was a kid, you know? Leave my mark that I was there. Proof that I ever existed."

Will nodded.

"I look at all the fake smiles from the people that are sick of running the same rat race but are too afraid to face it or say anything about it. Change is an emotion of fear. It all seems so pointless to me—always has. That's what I saw at a young age. That's why I was so rebellious. What is the point of all of this?"

"Bills have to be paid, food has to get on the table, and the kids go off to college. And let's not forget about braces," Will said. "Christenings, birthdays, proms, hopeful weddings, and of course, keeping the wife happy."

"It's a damn trap structured to keep us stupid and going at it." Collier raised his beer to Will. "But we're here now, and we should make the best of it. Let's stop worrying about work while we're away from work. Let's leave the assholes where they belong. Because we deserve this. We deserve to forget for a few days. Isn't that what we said during the drive here?"

"Yes, we did," Will said and settled deeper into the chair. "So much for not talking about it, huh? Anyway, this, right here, is way overdue."

"And the wife told you to go, remember that. There's no reason to feel guilty. You provide. And she told you to have a good time. That's up to us now." Collier looked at Will again. "We are in charge of our own happiness here and now, and I want to toss my 'I don't give two shits' into them woods somewhere and forget about them. Maybe I'll get lucky enough and an animal will pick it up, eat it, run far away from here, and crap it out somewhere even farther away."

"You have a way with words."

"So, let's make the best of it, yes?"

"And remember the deal." Will dug into his back pocket and pulled out his cell phone. "None of this nonsense while we're here. Two buds having some Buds and reminiscing. That's it."

"That's it. I'll drink to that too!"

The men clanked bottles, and each took a drink. Will put his phone away to avoid the temptation.

Collier sat back in his chair, took a swig from a half-empty bottle, and breathed in deeply the mountain air.

"Yes, this is wonderful."

Will nodded and then laughed.

Collier looked at him. "What's so funny?"

"I don't know. We've only been here two hours, haven't even unpacked, already bitched about work, and I've already started to feel guilty about leaving the family behind."

"Yeah, I was just thinking that, too, but I didn't want to say so after the macho bullshit speech we just gave each other."

They laughed together.

"I won't say anything if you don't."

Collier zipped his mouth.

"I've been watching those clouds out of the corner of my eye for the last five minutes. Look at that, would you?" Will pointed to the valley beneath them. "Look at those storm clouds rolling. They look vicious, no?"

"They do. That's anger in the sky."

"They were all the way down in that valley, but the storm looks like it's climbing the mountainside."

"Yeah, I hadn't noticed that until you just said something. It seems they're pushing up fast."

"Really fast."

The men watched for a moment. The clouds rolled, black and threatening. The trees around them began to sway, bringing a chill. Soon it would be on top of them.

Will looked at the large overhang that covered the porch, and he deemed it safe. "Did I ever tell you how much I love watching the rain? Storms are amazing and calming."

"I do, too," Collier said and stretched his neck. "Sometimes I sit in the car to hear the pitter-patter on the roof. Not to harp, but that's when I reflect the most, and I often wonder what my life would be like if I were more like you."

"Stop it, would you? You're making me feel uncomfortable. You know that."

"But it's true. I've always been the loser. The lazy one that caused trouble—and didn't give a damn when I did."

"You were a kid."

"I'm not necessarily focusing on that, but still, I knew well enough. I was doing things I never told you about because I didn't want to hear you lecture me."

"Like what?"

"I was robbing people when I couldn't find work."

Will's head snapped up quickly as he looked at his friend. "You what?"

"I know, I'm ashamed, but I needed to get it off my chest. Let you know how messed up I can really be."

"Why wouldn't you just come to me?"

"Because I'm too damn proud, and I didn't care at the time. My moral compass is dialed down to the lowest setting. And I figured your money is your money, not mine. Your success, not mine. My burden, not yours. Why in the hell should I visit that on you?"

"That's the most insulting thing you've ever said to me. Think about this for a moment. I'd have to bail your ass out of jail and then pay to defend you. That would have cost me ten times the amount rather than just giving you what you needed. It's only money, Collier. If I ever hear of you doing that again, I'll personally kick your ass."

"With the violin? Or will you lull me into a trance first with an acapella tune?"

"Go ahead and joke. That's some serious stuff right there."

"I know. It has been a while since I've done anything like that."

"How long is a while?"

"Since I found the new job I'm in. It's been around six months."

"Stupid," Will said. "Just stupid."

The conversation had raged like the approaching storm and let up as the heavy curtain of water fell. It came down in blinding sheets, stifling their argument, stealing their awe. The wind blew debris around, stirring things up in strong blasting gusts. Trees rocked back and forth, their limbs creaking as they strained to make yet another stand against Mother Nature.

The ground beneath their feet groaned, and the wood cabin rattled behind and above them.

"What the hell was that?" Collier asked and stood.

Will stood, too, unsure. "Maybe we should get inside."

A noise boomed and rolled like thunder all around them, shaking the ground, knocking the beer out of Collier's hand and leaving both men to struggle to retain their footing.

"That wasn't thunder," Collier shouted. "You felt the ground rumble. You had to have felt it!"

"I felt it."

"I think there might have been a rockslide or something. Did you look to see what was behind the cabin?"

"As far as I saw it was just woods. The land is flat back there."

"You sure? No mountain? I don't want to be inside the cabin and getting buried alive by an avalanche."

"Yeah, I'm pretty sure. The ground was flat as far as I could see."

What sounded like a stampede of horses filled the air, and the men looked around, trying to see where it was coming from. It was all around them, but they could see nothing. The driving rain and beating wind nearly blinded them as they fought the elements.

The men exchanged glances, their arms raised, forearms across the foreheads to help shield their eyes. Neither one of them scared easily, but whatever was going on certainly warranted concern.

"Do you think that cracking sound came from behind the cabin?" Will said.

"It sure sounded like it. Maybe it was trees falling? A small tornado might have touched down or something? Have you ever heard the sound of a tornado?"

"No."

"Damn. Me neither."

The rain, wind, and clouds dissipated as quickly as they had come. So had the sounds. It was so quiet, though neither man realized right away that the normal sounds of the forest had been stifled.

"We should go look," Collier said.

"Yeah, but that storm! I felt like I was in the middle of that funnel that took Dorothy away in the *Wizard of Oz*. It about gave me a heart attack. I was thinking it was the apocalypse and the second coming of Christ was upon us," Will said.

Collier shot Will a disapproving glance. "I don't want to get into a religious debate with you. That's off limits, too, with all the bullcrap things we spoke about before. We're here to relax. Christ ain't coming down to save your sorry ass—besides the fact that he doesn't even exist."

"Oh, He exists all right."

"Yeah, well then so does Santa—and that fat chick you screwed our senior year, if we're bringing up mythical creatures. Talk about taking one for the team!"

"Pure error in judgment, simpleton."

"Sheep that likes them plump."

Without a rebuttal, Will just laughed.

The men stepped off the porch and made their way around to the back of the cabin. They had to watch their footing with all the fallen refuse.

"Just listen to me for a second," Will said.

Collier rolled his eyes. "Oh, here we go."

"Suppose I'm wrong," Will said, unwilling to let up. "What have I lost?"

Collier sighed. "Nothing, I suppose. But go ahead and get it out. I know you're not going to shut up until you've said whatever it is that's on your mind."

"Suppose I'm right. What have you lost? Think about that. I mean really think about it."

"Forget it, Will. It went in one ear and right out the other. You won't scare me into believing in something that's just not there with your hypotheticals. You've been trying to recruit me into that cult for years, and it'll never happen. Live and let live, my friend. Embrace our differences."

"You know I have and always will. That doesn't mean I won't keep trying. I'm just worried about you is all."

"I worry about you, too. Stop following cults."

The men fell into silence as they stepped into the yard and found a sinkhole about thirty feet behind the cabin. The ground had swallowed anything that had been there before. The trees that circumvented the hole leaned inward, crossing as if to brace the hole from collapsing any further.

"Look at the tree over there, set back from the hole," Will said, pointing.

Collier looked, and they stared at a tree that was covered with locusts, the bark completely hidden by a massive amount of bugs. The insects jockeyed for position, climbing over one another, falling to the ground, and repeating. The tree trunk was alive with movement.

"Maybe they had a nest that was disturbed?"

"Maybe."

Collier moved forward and approached the hole with caution.

"I wonder how far down that goes."

"Careful, Collier. You don't know if that thing is done caving in, and I don't feel like fishing your ass out of there. I'd have a good mind to leave you until our vacation was over."

Collier ignored his friend's good advice, as he always did, and neared the sinkhole. He stood on his toes to get a look inside. It disappeared into blackness.

"It's pretty damn deep, and hot air is coming out of it. I can't even see the bottom. Come and look for yourself."

Will thought to protest but decided to look. It was intriguing, after all. He gazed into the massive hole, then backed away at the unsettling darkness. There was something unnatural about it. He began to pray silently.

"Do you have your cell phone on you? I left mine on the table," Collier said, his hand outstretched, assuming Will had it.

"Yeah, sure."

Will dug into his back pocket, pulled out his phone, and handed it over, praying all the while.

Collier took pictures of the trees crisscrossed over the hole, then of the locusts covering the tree. He then changed the setting to film. He turned on the light, braced himself against a tree, leaned over the hole, stuck out his arm, and oscillated, trying to film every portion of the collapse.

After about four minutes, Collier stopped film-ing, pushed himself upright, and flipped through the phone to access and watch the video.

They could hear the continuous sound of debris as it broke away inside the hole, but Collier's atten-tion remained glued to the glowing phone screen.

"That is not stable, Collier. You got your shot, now let's step away from that thing and we'll have a look at whatever is on the phone on the porch. I don't trust it. We need to call the authorities. I don't think us being in the cabin tonight is safe either. We can get a hotel room."

Collier watched the cell phone screen with deep scrutiny, again paying no attention to his friend and his warnings. His pupils shrank to pinpoints and his mouth hung open at what he saw.

"Oh my God! Are you fucking kidding me?"

Will hurried to his friend's side. "What? What is it?"

Collier dragged his finger across the screen and rewound the film about thirty seconds. Together, the men watched. Their faces moved closer to the screen, trying to figure out what they were looking at.

"Look," Collier said, and his finger shook over the image. "There's something climbing up."

"What?"

He paused the phone and handed it over to Will. "You tell me what."

Will watched it again, and the dark silhouette of a humanoid form and the glow of eyes from the camera lighting stared back at them.

"There's something in that hole," Will whispered. "Whatever it is, it's climbing up the wall!"

"Maybe it's an animal?"

"That's not a damn animal and you know it!"

"Then what?"

"It's a damn person! Look at the screen! It's a damn person!"

"That's not possible."

Just then a hand swung out of the hole. Taut fingers slammed into the soil and took root. The person emerged from the canyon, and all the men could do was stare, frozen by their fear.

CHAPTER 6

CAILEAN

Cailean's face hid deep in the shadow of her hood. The cloak fit as if it had been fashioned especially for her. Long enough to drag on the ground behind her, the sleeves hung loosely and allowed her ample freedom of movement.

She approached a sickened woman who was on her deathbed. The woman's soul was trapped inside her disease-ravaged body, desperate to break free, reaching out for death. Sunken eyes pleaded to Cailean, voice moaning, the spirit yearning to leave the vessel. The body had withered to almost nothing, carrying no strength apart from its tremendous will to live. The fight had gone on for years. But no longer. Her departure was near.

Her old, frail, age-spotted hands grabbed Cailean's cloak, but they easily slipped off. The woman just had no strength left. The energy had been sapped from her body, stolen away by the fight she'd lost with cancer. It had riddled her body and eaten at her from the inside. A body turned against itself. And it had taken its time doing so, too.

Years.

Her family had to care for her, watch her fade and become helpless in her pain, her thinking, and her indignity.

Gathered around her bedside now were five family members, varying in age. Cailean looked at the elderly man in the group. She would be coming for him soon. It would be less than six months' time. A heart so broken that it would allow disease to enter and destroy.

She turned her attention back to the woman in need.

"Your time has come," Cailean said, her voice a guttural groan that was meant to be sensitive. Understanding. Comforting. But it was none of those things. "I'm here for you. I'm going to give you the mercy you so desperately deserve."

She was here not as Cailean, for that was her human name. Now, she came as Death itself. Cailean was a name she had forgotten, erased from her mind—a name that had been taken away from her by Sariel.

As she worked, she sometimes thought about who she might be, but there was this giant void that followed her around like the darkness she dwelled in. It was a cavernous, flat, endless blackness, and it had every intention of keeping all its secrets.

She groused at the fleeting thought of who she really was.

If she could remember, she would know the deal she had made with Sariel was fair. It gave her the chance to escape who she was and what she had done. Her punishment had been minor compared to what it could have been. Although her sentence was a curse, it was also a blessing. Who she was in life had been a monster far worse than what she was now. In fact, she had been something far worse than the cancer that feasted upon that old woman.

The memory that eluded her was lost in exchange to give someone a chance at life . . . someone she had failed over and over again. Someone she had hurt, ignored, and abused. This someone was a person of great importance. She needed to prove her love to him, and there was no other way but to prove it through one final act of love.

The ultimate sacrifice.

Her life for his.

Her place here for eternity with these questions constantly plaguing her. A hunger that could never be satisfied.

She knew at the time she didn't deserve life and was therefore content with her decision. That's why she was here. That's why she was Death. But what she didn't know at the time was how uncomfortable she would be playing the role.

Screams.

Agony.

Begging.

Ceaseless needs.

Disorder.

Mercy.

Selflessness.

Unrelenting service.

She had since worn the cowl and ushered the dead, fulfilling her obligation of the interminable task. This assignment would plunder her body worse than it had Sariel's. The skin she wore on deadside was not designed to withstand the strain of this burden that had been placed on her. Her feet were already tired and raw, her back sore, her mind tangled in confusion and getting worse. The freezing cold and the darkness were her only protection and luxury. She tried to remain there as much as she could.

She was often scorned and seldom welcomed in what she had to do. It made no sense, yet she had to do it. She looked at her pale, clawed hands. That didn't make sense either. How did they get this way?

The task . . . over and over with no rest, a pre-programming of sorts; no explanation. Yet, as she worked in the moment, her desire to rest didn't exist.

There were so many like this dying woman in the bed. A moment to pause, to offer sympathy, to mourn, would only create chaos on deadside. Cailean needed to keep up. Stay ahead, listen to the voices that called out to her. There were so many, yet with her mind—if that was how she truly thought—she was able to organize and follow the ebb and flow . . . but only barely. She was still learning.

Cailean, Death Incarnate, reached her pale hand out, and the black cloth that covered it fell away. Her fingernails were long and sharp and her breathing a frightening wheeze, yet her touch was gentle and comforting as she took hold of the old woman with the outstretched hand. Cailean gave a soft pull.

With that, the old woman's soul ejected from the body. Slid out like a baby being born. The terrible, steady, flatline beep of a failed heart echoed in the background. The old woman's kind eyes betrayed confusion at the moment. A natural shock. She stared at Death, and as a combination of terror mixed with relief spread across her face, she wept gently.

Cries of the family wailed over the beep, and the old woman went to turn around to see if she could console the anguish of those who had come to be by her side in her final moments. But Death reached her hand out again and took the old woman by the shoulder, keeping her from seeing their grief.

"You don't need to see that," Cailean said. "You are to walk with me now. I'll take you where you need to go."

"I don't understand."

"You have died. Disease has ravaged your body, and the doctors could not afford you any more time. I have come to escort your soul to the other side."

The old woman shrugged off Cailean's hold and looked back. Cailean was unsure what she could see.

"But, my family, what about them?"

Maybe she could see what Cailean saw. Everything on the other side that had to do with this moment. It was as if she could step in and out of time without being detected. A one-way mirror to protect her presence.

"They will mourn, and they will heal. But most importantly, your suffering has now come to an end. I have shown you the mercy you so desperately wanted. Now come with me."

"No, I want to be with them!"

"You cannot."

"I want to see my grandson that was just born. A boy. The first to carry on the last name."

"They will teach him all about you."

"No, you don't understand. I am not ready to die. Why would you take me from them?"

"You were sick, riddled with cancer, wrought with pain and suffering. Tremendous suffering and pain. Your soul reached out to me, called across the great beyond and begged for mercy. You were so desperate in your plea, I could no longer ignore it. Pity. I have given that to you."

"I don't want what you have given me! I want to go back."

"There is no going back. You have died, leaving behind only pain and the misery of a body that has outlived its use. Those broken hearts are not your responsibility. That is what comes with death. The living must experience, endure, and prepare themselves on a subconscious level for what is to come for them, too."

"What is to come?"

"Me."

"How could you?"

"How could I not?"

The old woman turned her head and seemingly saw her lifeless body lying in the hospital bed. The people that surrounded her wept, looked up to the heavens for answers they would never find.

"There are no answers up there, are there? It is only here."

"There are answers. You must get to them, and only then will you be free."

Death held on tight and pulled the woman along, no longer listening to the old woman's protests. It continued. The process. Over and over again.

Blame.

Fear.

Hate.

Misjudgment.

Why couldn't people understand that she was there to help them, guide them, get them through their time of need? Without her they would be lost, left to wander the flat plains in search of the way to the other side.

The coarse ground dug into Cailean's feet as it had for the past day, and the pain seeped from her feet and into her heart. A heart full of pity, despair, misunderstanding and, like so many others, a question she couldn't quite grasp. What was the meaning behind her existence?

Her tasks?

But being in service of the people distracted her from finding conclusions to such questions and even took them from her mind. So, she went about her duty to usher the dead, not remembering.

Distracted.

Motivated by the unknown.

Body hurting.

Time ticking.

Never stopping.

Tick, tock.

There, in the distance, was a bridge with a candlelit lamp atop two vertical posts. Although the light flickered and was dim, it was forever burning. It illuminated the way to the other side. The slow-moving River of Life and Death rolled beneath the bridge, the sound soothing. Encouraging even. This was the only part where Cailean found appreciation in her duty.

"Go on now," Death said.

The bridge allowed the person to cross over and forget the trauma of life, to leave their troubles and concerns behind. To find rest at last and hopefully to understand Death and her plight.

Cailean let go of the woman's hand. As the elderly lady stepped onto the bridge the old wooden slats creaked beneath her weight.

"How could you do this to me?" The old woman looked over her shoulder and scowled at Death. Death turned away. She could already hear the next person in need of freedom from their bondage of pain. So, she set off to travel the endless road of service to humanity in their worst, most-vulnerable, and unpredictable time.

Unappreciated and feared, she had already come to expect the reaction. It was trying and difficult to understand at first, but it was something to never forget. The only place to contemplate was in the darkness of the hood that covered her pale face. It was nice there. Comforting. But the moments were brief. She had so much work to do.

Why did she wear this black thing anyhow?

She looked over her shoulder and the old woman was gone. She had successfully crossed over to the other side.

Cailean's attention swung in the direction her sore feet took her, the path dark and pleasant. The voice that called out to her—like most—was loud. So loud she couldn't think of anything else but getting to that voice and helping its owner.

The tasks needed to be carried out. No option. A must. And although there was something appealing about the sound of the rushing water, a place she'd like to stay, she didn't have time to enjoy it. Tasks that needed to be done pushed her along.

Invisible hands.

A shove.

Go.

"Excuse me," a voice said from behind her. She turned and looked at the bridge. The woman had gone, but there, to Cailean's surprise, between the lanterns, stood a boy. The candlelight cast his image in an eerie, flickering shadow. But she didn't need the light to see him, so she squinted and saw him in the darkness.

He wore black shoes laced high up to his shins, striped stockings, and a plain dress.

"I need to have a word with you, lady," the boy said.

"Have you been lost this whole time?"

"No," he said. "I've just arrived. Why do you ask?"

"The way that you're dressed. It seems you're from a generation long gone."

The anguished voice cried out again, and she looked in its direction.

"I'm from a generation much older than what you probably imagine. And that voice you hear calling out to you? Never mind that for right now."

"I sense no soul in you," Death said. "Who are you and what are you doing here?"

"I don't have a soul like a human. But I have come a great distance and with a great purpose. I come with wisdom, bravery, and the truth. To explain, I'm going to need a few minutes of your time."

Cailean looked over her shoulder again and into the far-away blackness. The place where she needed to go.

"Believe me, they can wait, and this cannot," the boy said. "The time we need here is merely a millisecond on the other side. You've been told time moves differently here? Much slower?"

"Why would I need to be told? I know that. I've experienced it, have prior knowledge. For I am Death."

"Yes, of course you are, forgive me."

She had never seen this child, and she was curious about him. She hadn't placed him here and wondered how he managed to navigate the vast black space she traveled. Did he have special eyesight like her?

"Did you set out to find me?" she asked, having forgotten some of the details he had already provided.

"Yes, I've come looking for you. I knew I would find you here, at the bridge. This is where you take the ones that are ready to cross over."

She pulled her hood back and looked upon the boy that wasn't a soul and wasn't a demon. No, he was something much different. A faint familiarity tried to insert itself into her consciousness, but something blocked it.

"Come closer to me," she said.

The boy did as she asked and stood in front of her. She reached out her cold, dead hand and caressed his cheek. Her eyes moved closer, curious, and her labored breathing halted as she smelled him. The sniff was long, and she held it.

"Hmm." Her inspection revealed nothing. "Where do you come from?" she asked.

"The Valley."

"The Valley of Death?"

"You've heard of it?"

"If I am Death, and it is my job to sort the souls, then why wouldn't I know about it? The damned have their place, too, you know. Why do you question me about such strange things?"

"Because you are not who you think you are, and your knowledge about this place is so little that it puts you in danger."

Cailean scoffed, pulled the hood over her head, and turned away. "You found your way in; I'm sure you'll find your way out. I have work to do."

"I can find my way easy enough, but I'm not leaving, and neither are you. I've come to help you," the boy said.

Death stopped. "You say what it is I'm going to do as if you have some authority over me, especially here?"

"For your own good, of course. Your human name was Cailean," the boy said. "And you had a son. His name is Beau. He is still very much alive, thanks to you."

Death turned around, pulled the hood back again, and moved close to the boy. Her dead eyes danced back and forth. "What is your name?"

"Keir."

"What is your purpose?"

"I serve the dead."

"As do I."

"Yes. But I help the sinful souls remember who they are. I help prepare them to face their demons. Send them to their eternal damnation."

"You take them after I deliver them?"

"Something like that, yes."

"Tell me more."

"I would, but it is irrelevant, and time shouldn't be spent on that. I work in the cabins. Use the books inside the Akashic Halls."

"The Akashic Halls?" Death sank into herself to try to find the answer to another elusive question. Unsatisfied, she looked at Keir. "What books?"

"A book you are mentioned in. But what needed to be done was never fulfilled."

"Why?"

"Because you were fooled into believing this is what you are supposed to be. I assure you, it is not."

Cailean stared. Her dead eyes held no expression, but there was something there. Invisible curiosity.

"Your memory has been altered," Keir said. "I am here to help you remember. To give you a chance to break free from what you are doing. This is not your work. This is not your design. This is not your place."

Cailean rubbed her chin. Her dead eyes searched for life, but here there was only death.

"If you will listen, I can help you," he said.

"Why would you interfere with my operation?"

"Like I said, this is not the way things are supposed to be. I was sent to help you remember. Getting you to remember is of grave importance."

The sound of the beckoning voice turned her attention again.

"You need to listen to me," Keir said. "Not that voice in the distance."

"Who sent you?"

"Twyla."

Cailean allowed herself to sink deep into a memory that held nothing but orders and procedures on how to serve the dead. She shook her head.

"I've never heard of her."

"She's another who works in the cabins. Her job is like mine, but she has superiority. She needs to move you on."

"But you said you usher the sinful."

"We do."

"Am I one of the sinful? Is that your accusation?"

"Yes."

"No, that can't be right."

"It is."

"If that is true, then I am safer here, doing what I am doing for the people. It will give me a chance to make up for whatever it is I have done."

"No," Keir said. "You are not. That's a folly. You're in danger of the things that are to come after you when they discover your weaknesses."

"I am Death. What can they do to me?"

Keir kicked at the ground. "They know you are uncertain, just dropped into this post with little direction. Vulnerable. Powers weak. I promise you, they will come for you. They will create disorder and will move people in death where they don't belong, messing with the balance and order of things. Imagine a sinful sent over the bridge rather than into the Valley. Think how disastrous that could be! How about an innocent sent to the forest, lost in the Valley of Death with no one to protect them from the things that roam the woods. There are vile things there! Now, I want you to try and imagine what would happen to the innocent." Keir shook his head. "Your post is responsible for the balance and order of deadside. They know that. I hate to tell you that you could never hope to keep up, and when you have lost control, that is when they will strike."

"Who is they?"

"Just more names that mean nothing to you. I need you to listen to what I have to say so I can help free you."

"What is freedom?"

"Freedom is what you will obtain when you have broken the bonds of serving here." Keir opened his arms. "Freedom from the lies you are controlled by."

"If you come with the truth as you say, name one thing."

"The true bearer of Death cannot remove their robe. It is a part of them. A part of the office and a way to protect its bearer."

Cailean pulled the robe over her head and dropped it at her feet. She was nude but had no shame. Only surprise that she wasn't inextricably connected to the garment. "What's this? Are you trying to trick me?"

"No tricks. I'm here to deliver the truth," Keir said and removed a duffel bag from his back. He set clothing on the ground for Cailean to change into. He took the robe and put it on. It hung off his body, four sizes too big.

"You see? Just fake memories covered in black linen and lies. Nothing more. You were chosen as a puppet to do someone's bidding because he wished to no longer do it. Fooled you into the role. I admit that you weren't very nice in life, but you don't deserve this sentence. It is far worse than the Valley."

Cailean reached out and touched Keir again. She caressed his skin, and it felt alive. Warm almost. There was something special about the boy.

"I want you to know everything you need to know, and then you will go," he said, allowing her touch to linger.

"Go where?"

"To where I need to send you. To where Twyla says you belong."

CHAPTER 7

AKASHIC HALLS

"You say you must go, but yet you still stand here," Sariel said.

"Because I'm hoping to talk some sense into you." There was a look of hope in Twyla's eyes. "Trust me that the path you are traveling on now is dangerous. You should abandon your quest and be more careful to keep your distance from the people. Their human curiosity has rubbed off on you, and it is leading you astray, putting all of us in grave danger."

"Danger from what?"

"You, Sariel. Danger from you. You will destroy all that you love."

"I intend to destroy only that which is in my way."

"That is my concern, and you're not listening to me or yourself."

"I have heard my words and yours. My vision is clear, and the circles you think I am running in are merely me finding my way through the unknown," Sariel said. "I have a yearning I must satisfy. I wish you would understand. I beg you to walk with me if you wish to be a part of my discovery."

Sariel turned and walked away, unsure if Twyla would follow him. Never had he seen her so defiant.

Then the sound of her feet following his inserted a sense of relief within, dissolving his momentary doubt.

"I'll look at the left side, and you look at the right. It should help cut the time in half."

Twyla continued to walk the halls with Sariel, aimlessly searching for what would be hours if it were to be compared to human time. Here, a day was more than six months of mortal time; sleep was unnecessary, although one might indulge every now and then just to take a break.

But, being here, inside the Valley within the Akashic Halls, didn't change the fact that Sariel was about 6,000 years old. Spawned just after the creation of man, his first love was tending to the Garden. But the bliss didn't last and was never intended to. Tainted by the shadow of sin . . . like this place—it would never be the same.

A snake.

An apple.

Curiosity.

Bite.

Sin.

Often he thought about returning to the Garden to see what it looked like, but he could imagine that the rotten touch of death had killed everything and it had long ago decayed away, leaving no remnants of what was once perfect.

Sariel scanned the spine of each book, names embossed onto the leather. He looked at Twyla and saw she wasn't paying attention to the books. She was looking at her feet, slowing her pace.

"Can you look at the books on the right? I'll go through what's on the left," Sariel repeated.

"We aren't going to find anything, Sariel," Twyla said and started to fall behind. Each step she took was filled with pain and struggle and a lack of desire to carry on with him. Her voice was unable to hide her fight and unwillingness to continue much longer.

"I'm certain we're going to find something. We just have to keep looking. Remain diligent."

"No," Twyla said and stopped. "I can't do this. I don't want to do this. Have you ever thought we're not going to find anything?"

"No."

"Well, we're not, because you wrote all of these. Every single book that is in here—you wrote it, Sariel. Don't you remember?"

"Of course I remember!"

"How did you do it, Sariel? How did you write all of these? Look at them. There are millions."

He looked at her, indifferent, bothered that his search had been halted by meaningless questions.

"What do you mean how did I do it, Twyla?"

"Where did you get your information from? All those millennia writing these books, tirelessly putting messages down through drawings like parables to one's life. Doing all that work for us. The angels who serve you here in the Valley."

"How does this bring me closer to the answer I seek?"

"How, Sariel? Answer me."

"You don't tell me what to do, woman."

"No," Twyla said and looked at Sariel's feet. "No one tells you what to do. That, right there, is part of the problem."

"Let them send someone then. I don't care. If you really need to know who told me, why don't you go and—"

"By whom!"

"Angelina. You know that. I need not remind you, or is it that you just wanted me to say it?"

"And do you still hear the commands she sends?"

"Of course. You know our work is never done."

"The commands are to be obeyed." Twyla rubbed her chin. "You haven't been writing what you are told?"

"No. Can't you see how tired I have grown? My hands can hardly grip the coal, my feet can barely carry me, and my mind is so busy that I can no longer concentrate on such things."

"Ask Him for help. Surely, He will ease what ails you. Or are you too proud?" Twyla turned away.

"How dare you!"

"How dare you not!"

"Has He eased what ails you?"

"I speak often. Yes, do you not remember what you saw in the mirror? You have gotten away from doing that. Disconnected yourself, concerned yourself with human things far beyond death. I know it. You are so curious about them. It is no wonder why you walk around with such affliction."

Sariel looked down at the blood pooled at his feet, telling the story of his hard labor.

"I have grown accustomed to it."

"You shouldn't have to," Twyla said and looked over her shoulder in disgust. "I must play and look the part. That is why I wear the old skin suit. I can become what I want to be when necessary. You cannot because you like to grovel in your misery."

"You pretend to know what makes me tick?"

"You are so far gone, I wouldn't know where to begin."

"We have played the part since the Creation. Six thousand years of service, struggle, unanswered questions, and a measure of uncertainty is a long time to carry on so blindly. Maybe we are playing the fools' game. I think it is time for us to rest."

"There is no rest for us. You took this post, and I followed you. I have been assigned to that cabin, left there since the beginning, dishing out your lessons to the people who come. Hoping night after night I would see you. I waited so long and have been disappointed. I wasn't expecting this. This is the last time I'll implore you to stop this search. Nothing good can come from it. Do you understand that?"

Sariel stared, his silence an insertion of discomfort and tension. Twyla spoke with a need to fill the gap.

"I do this because I believe the message must be sent," Twyla said. "I believe in the messages of the messenger and never thought I'd see him so confused or even worse: Have a willingness to quit; to walk away without a measure of care about what sort of devastation he leaves behind in his wake. There will be great destruction with little hope of repair."

"You speak as if you're clairvoyant now! You insult me!"

"I speak the truth I see. Your feelings mean nothing to me until you veer off this wayward path. Do you hear me? You are not walking on the right path, Sariel!"

"Do you think you can threaten me by not talking to me, accusing me of causing destruction when you sit in a chair by the fireside? You occupy a throne of comfort, have a table to rest your elbows on, and yet you have the nerve to lecture someone who is tired of being a serf? Forever walking, never to cease?"

"You misconstrue my words. Twist them so you can carry out your plan with a clear conscience. It will not end that way."

"You regard these people, their life's stories, through visions and creations of my own!" He held up his gnarled hands. "Written by these twisted things. All created to bring them discomfort in the way you tell the story, woven like a master manipulator."

Twyla's eyes danced around and searched Sariel's.

"What happened to you, Sariel?"

"You are a storyteller who reads from a book that I author! I am something so much more!"

"You are what?"

"Not to be trifled with, woman!" He turned away, curled into his own anger. Rage competed with unquenchable satisfaction, threatening to boil over. The cloak hung off his body, his shoulders hardly thicker than a clothes hanger. "I am free now, and you are envious."

"No. You are envious of the people. You forget you are a servant of the dead. Your actions are going to bring you and others great misfortune."

"Again, you stake claim to divination? Is that your play?"

"If you could only hear yourself, Sariel. You sound sick."

"I hear and feel just fine. It was *seeing* that I wasn't able to do before this day."

"Love is tough, and it leaves me with little choice," Twyla said.

The concern in her words seemed genuine, and Sariel felt the rising anger start to abate. "What do you claim to know about love?" Embarrassment settled in and bit down, pushing the conflicting feelings away.

"That right now it hurts more than anything I've felt or experienced in my very long life. You are deserting your post," she said. "Leaving behind all those who have followed you. Leaving them—us—exposed. You are ignoring your commands to usher the dead and inform us about the damned we must deal with. There's no throne here for me to sit on, no rest for me when my elbows are on a table as you suggest. There are only the sinful for me to strip bare, and it breaks my heart; it does not harden it as it has done to yours."

"I am doing this because I can no longer endure," Sariel said. "I'm so tired. Plain and simple. Why can't you understand that?"

"We don't tire, Sariel. That is all in here," Twyla said and tapped her temple. "We require no rest. That is the way we are. What you are doing here and now is a choice you are making. One to defy. Remember what happened to all those who defied Him. Please don't do that. Not to yourself, and not to me."

"I need no reminding of what He can do, and what I do has nothing to do with you. At least not anymore." Sariel held up his gnarled hands. His twisted, grotesque fingers wiggled. "What they did . . . the ones that started all this . . . they have done this to me, and they hide like cowards. All because of defying a simple rule within the Garden. But they will have their day, won't they?"

"They will."

"So, maybe today I will have mine. I wish to destroy them all."

"You cannot. Your authority over the dead is diminishing with each passing moment. Your choices will have consequences. Repercussions you will have to answer for. How many times am I to say this? You don't ask how. You just keep talking about yourself and your needs."

"You can say it as many times as you'd like. My needs are first right now, yes. They won't find me until I want to be found."

"Like the sins of the sinful won't find them either? We know the order. We know your words carry anger but little merit."

Sariel removed his hood. His scrunched, wrinkled face; long, drooping ears; and encased, sad eyes implored for understanding. Not through compassion and gentleness, rather, through the ire behind his stance.

"Don't you see that I am no regular man caught up in the ways of sin and corruption? These damn people! It is the same, one after the other. I am on a quest . . . a hunt to gain an understanding of who I really am. Me! There is understanding somewhere in here, in these halls, waiting for me to discover it."

"You are on a fool's errand, and you've become someone I don't know."

"I am a simple man who once tended to the Garden. That man I have long ago forgotten. I've let him go. But I wish to be him again."

"You and so many others, Sariel. But you will never be. The Garden is gone. Sin and death are what remain in this world we tend."

Twyla shook her head and walked away. Time had done her no favors in the appearance she now embodied.

"Take your time, find out who you are then," she said. "Tie that noose correctly so it breaks the fall."

"What is that supposed to mean?"

Twyla paused but didn't face Sariel.

"You will see, just as you know they will come. They will want to know why things have stopped.

I am afraid for you and afraid for me. But you will continue on this new path. You've made that abundantly clear. There is no talking you out of it."

"Someone is there, in my stead."

"And knows nothing about what you do or did to her! These . . . sinners will continue to come here, and all who run the cabins will not know what to do. They will not know who is sitting in front of them. Chaos will come and override the order, and that will be on you."

Twyla took several more angry steps.

"Don't you put this all on me!"

She whirled around. "But you are Death. You are their end."

"I am no longer."

"You are and always will be. You will discover that is an inescapable truth." Twyla stomped off.

"Don't you just walk away from me!" Sariel shouted, but Twyla continued. "How dare you turn your back and just leave me like this! Does what we had mean nothing to you?"

Still she walked, and he thought to run to her, grab her, and shake some sense into her. But he remained, sitting back in anger, watching her fade away until she was out of sight, most likely returning to her post at the cabin. Ever so loyal.

Sariel lashed out. He swept an arm across a bookshelf and the books scattered onto the floor and into the pools of his blood.

He panted from his outburst, tired but determined. There had to be something about him within these halls. Who he was. Who he might be. Or might have been. Where he should go. What he should do.

So, he moved onward.

His pace was much slower now that he had to look at both sides of the hall. The "S" files seemed to carry on forever. But the long, winding halls in front of him were nothing new. The road he walked to serve the people was so much greater. This would be over soon.

He pressed on, bothered by Twyla's words, distracted even. Her message carried something ominous, obviously meant to deter him. But he wouldn't be persuaded. He would remain firm. As he had always known, there was a reason and outcome for everything. He had been writing about it from the commands that came from above for so long that he believed a book about himself had made it into the Akashic Halls, penned by someone unknown, the contents a mystery soon to be resolved.

He found himself wandering without looking at the editions, lost in the vastness of the catalog the imps were responsible for tending to. The book could be miles away or in the next case over. He didn't know, and so he continued his search.

Zipping past Sariel from one row to another, an imp appeared and then disappeared into another hallway. While it busied itself with its task, Sariel latched onto a moment of hope.

"I need you," he called out. "It is Sariel, and I need you to help me locate a book."

The imp's small, clawed hands grabbed the wooden shelf, his body hidden, but Sariel could hear the beat of his wings. Slowly, with caution, the small, fire-red imp peered around the corner and locked eyes with Sariel.

It came out of hiding and flew to him, hovering in front of him. Sariel raised an arm, bent it at the elbow, and held it out. The imp landed near his wrist and folded its wings. The creature hunched and looked into his eyes, awaiting a command.

"I believe there is a book in here with my name on it. Do you know of such a thing?".

The imp with the bone-mask face stared at Sariel, its expression like stone, but Sariel saw something in it. Was it surprise from the question?

"I asked you if you know of such a book."

The imp nodded.

"I need you to help me find it. Now."

It took flight, hovered, turned away, and motioned for Sariel to follow.

"Keep pace," Sariel said, his legs tired, his feet hurting. The imp had to know something. He saw it in its face when he first asked, could feel it in its hesitation. Sariel could sense the electricity coursing through his veins. He moved quickly, keeping up with the creature so as not to lose him in this giant maze.

After many twists and turns, the imp flew up high, almost to the ceiling, much higher than Sariel could easily see, and pulled out a thin, tattered book. It gave the volume to Sariel, touched his ancient face with admiration, hugged his neck, and flew away.

Pressed into the cover, seared by a branding iron, the shadow of Sariel's name contrasted with the book's dusty cover. Sariel almost wept. He knew it. His departure from his post had been written, known long before he arranged it to happen, driven by something unseen, propelled by his own distaste and curiosity of what he saw and what he was becoming. He was destined to be something else. He just knew it. This was a pivotal moment.

He struggled to sit. The descent to the floor made his joints crack and groan in objection. He placed the book on his lap. His nervous fingers caressed the impression, felt the leather. They began to shake as he reached to open the cover only to find a moment of doubt.

Maybe Twyla was right and he was testing fate. Was it possible he'd toyed with something that should be left alone? But the need to know was impossible to ignore. The leather groaned as if it were a long-lost vault finally cracked open, having meant to be locked away and hidden in plain sight forever.

The cover fell open, and particles of leather trailed into his lap. There was a stack of pages inside. Fragile and yellowed by time, the very first page contained few words written in fancy letters and centered on the page:

Sariel, The Fifth Angel
See Apollyon

Sariel turned to the next page, and it was blank. He flipped through the rest of the pages. All blank.

"What is this?"

He struggled to stand.

"What is the meaning of this?" he shouted, his voice no longer tired. His pained echo filled the hallways and carried on for miles, heard by every serving imp.

CHAPTER 8

THE PIT

Will and Collier watched the red hand slam the ground and sink its fingers into the dirt. Glass crystals formed around the puncture holes, and the muscles in the forearm worked to pull the body out of the sinkhole.

The men stared, stunned. The thing they caught on camera stood up, naked and breathing heavily. He—they supposed it was a man of some sort—brushed himself off and looked at them with a smile. No, it was a grin. The contortion of the mouth told them that this was a wiseguy, up to no good.

Fire-red skin sizzled, blistered, peeled, and smoked. Piercing yellow eyes darted back and forth between Collier and Will, clearly searching for something. As the man advanced, the friends backed up the few steps they could manage. The being's head smoldered, but hair started to grow in.

These unimaginable events were enough to keep the friends firmly in place, silenced and backed into a corner. They were frozen in a moment of bewilderment with terror personified standing right in front of them.

"What is your name?" the man asked, pointing at Collier. His voice was deep, gravelly, and apparently so hot his throat belched fumes like an incinerator.

"Collier," the terrified tourist said with a tongue that stuck to the roof of his mouth. "Collier Steadman."

"A unique name in its own right. Interesting that its meaning indicates coal or burning," the man said with a sinister chuckle. Charred skin continued to fall off, revealing a white, fleshy tone underneath. "I like that name for you. It is fitting. What about your friend? What is his name?"

Collier looked at Will then back at the smoldering man. "His name is Will Garavuso."

The man sniffed the air around Will, keeping his distance.

"A man of God?"

Now it was Will's turn to look at Collier. Collier was lost within the statements and questions and weird actions of the man who stood before them. The transformation he was undergoing before their eyes was unexplainable, odd, and petrifying.

A man had emerged from a giant hole in the ground, practically on fire. Yet his flesh cooled and revealed normal skin beneath. His hair inexplicably grew back, and he spoke exactly as they did.

"Yes, I believe in the Lord."

"As do I," the strange man said. "I've seen Him with my own eyes, if you can believe that." He raised his brows and that smile came back.

"What does He look like?" Will asked. The question seemed stupid after it came out of his mouth.

The man laughed. "Nothing like your depictions suggest."

"Are you—"

"Hungry?" The man rubbed his stomach. "Yes." He whistled and made a strange animal sound. A boar came out of the thicket and charged. The smoldering man grabbed it, lifted it over his head, and slammed it on the ground. The body split open from the fearsome force.

The man dropped to his knees and ate the thing down to the bone, cooking the meat as he held it. Covered in animal blood, he stood, licked his fingers, and said, "It's rude that I have asked your names, but you have not asked mine. So, which one of you is going to ask me what my name is?"

The men remained quiet, disorder within their auras, their senses of logic collapsed into the impossibility of the things they'd just witnessed.

"I'll make this easy. How about who I am?"

The men continued to look at him, at each other, and then back at him. Dread kept them nearly unresponsive as their minds tried to figure out what, exactly, it was they were looking at.

"Collier, do you want to know what I'm doing here?" He laughed. "You've always sought trouble." He winked and whispered, "You may have met your match."

Collier stiffened.

"So, do you want to know or not?"

Collier nodded, his eyes glass balls, his head on a swivel, his jaw dangling open. The bravado he'd had when he hung over the sinkhole was no more. He was reduced to a speechless child.

The smoldering man looked at the forest around him, up at the sky. "Beautiful." He closed his eyes and inhaled. "Breathtakingly beautiful."

Still steaming, the animal's blood boiling, the man reached his hand out and clapped Collier's shoulder. He said with a harsh laugh, "Never mind these questions for you. That would ruin the fun of what's to transpire here."

Collier snapped out of it and cringed, leaning as far away as he could. His hand brushed at his shoulder with a fierce attempt to remove embers that burned him.

Will rushed his friend, slapped at the smoking clothing, and helped him take it off. The imprint of the man's hand had burnt all the way through and onto the flesh beneath. It was red and had already begun to blister, though the touch had lasted less than a fraction of a second.

"You're burnt badly," Will said. "Don't touch it!"

Collier bent over and held his arm, his teeth clamped together, his lips peeled back from the pain, his eyes watering.

"And you are a nonbeliever, Collier." The man chuckled. "I can smell it. It carries a certain odor. Not quite like the brimstone I am exposed to, but an odor nevertheless. Unmistakable and undeniable. Imagine rejection having a stink. That's what you have."

"I believe!" Collier shouted.

The smoldering man started to laugh deep in his throat. Collier quivered at the guttural sound, forgetting his pain for the moment. A hand, no longer beet red but still hot, reached out and took Collier by the face. The fingers squeezed, and the skin the hand touched sizzled, the veins in Collier's face burned black. His mouth opened in an attempt to scream, but the man raised the other hand and snapped his fingers.

"You can't proclaim belief when it's convenient for you. That's not how that works."

Hundreds of locusts flew from the tree, their wings beating the air with an ear-piercing buzz, and they swarmed Collier's face, covered his body like the trunk of the tree, and descended into his mouth.

The man let him go, and Collier fell, convulsing on the ground, foaming at the mouth. The man from the pit turned his attention to Will, who managed to take another step away.

"Your will is strong. It was instilled when you were young, wasn't it?"

"Yes," Will said and looked at Collier. In this moment he wished he'd never come here. That he had just put up with the daily grind; complaints and wishes of something better be damned. Instead, an act of kindness and love had turned against him, and he may have been responsible for killing his best friend.

"Don't worry. You have the protection of your belief, and I cannot touch you. Those are the rules."

"A demon?"

"Something like that. The particulars make no difference in this moment. I suppose you'd agree.

You have your protection. Settle in and enjoy it. But watch what I can do to your friend, for you cannot stop me."

Will's eyes widened, and he again looked at Collier, who continued to writhe, his face swollen and blue. A sick gurgle bubbled out of his mouth.

Will knelt next to Collier. His hands hovered over his wretched friend. He wanted to help but didn't know what to do.

"Just be thankful that isn't you. Faith has its privileges." The smoldering man pulled at his chin. "No, I don't think that's the right word. 'Advantages' might be more accurate. Let's say it has its advantages."

Those words weren't enough to make Will relax. The things he saw, what was happening to Collier—it was too much. The man with the fuming, fire-red skin had emerged from the deep pit, his searing touch and cooling factor a mystery. The being's unearthly control over a wild animal and the way he rent it in seconds and devoured it in an equal amount of time was dumbfounding. Will's oldest friend on the ground with bugs inside his body, shaking and now spitting white frothy foam from his mouth.

This wasn't real.

"Wake up, wake up!"

"This is real, believer."

If Will were to run, would he make it?

"Not to civilization," the man said as if he could read his mind, hear his thoughts. Or maybe it was the body language, the darting of Will's eyes that he was reading?

"My name is Apollyon."

Will stood up and backed away, his mouth agape with a word in the form of an accusation caught somewhere deep in his throat, unable to come out.

For some reason, his mind wandered to the conversation he'd had with Collier before they reached the pit. His words weren't funny at all. He meant it when he said he was worried about his friend, and maybe his soul sensed the coming of Apollyon. The apocalypse had indeed come, started right here, in the middle of nowhere behind a cabin he just so happened to have rented. If he couldn't stop it here, sure enough, it would spread like a wildfire.

"From your reaction, I surmise you've heard of me?"

"Yes, of course. Revelation."

That same devious smile revealed itself again.

"Why . . . why have you come?" Will said.

"Good question, but one whose answer remains to be seen. Try something else."

"If I were to ask you a question, how would I know what you say is the truth?"

"Because I have nothing to hide from you, Believer Will. You already know that though, don't you? How I have no authority over you?"

"Yes."

Apollyon laughed and then winked at Will. Then his laugh stopped, and his smile faded in an instant.

"Are the end times here? Has it begun?"

"There was this man who came to me, after the earth peeled apart, splitting right where my shackles were embedded into the rock wall. They fell off, and I was free. The man was pleasantly dressed and nice enough, I suppose. He made me an offer and conveyed his terms through a messenger—the voice I heard came from one of those locusts, and it told me what to do."

"But you are the king of the locusts."

"Indeed I am."

"What did it tell you to do?"

"You are funny, Will. To think someone like me would answer to someone like you. Surprises abound. Like him." Apollyon pointed at Collier.

Collier went still; his eyes rolled toward the back of his head, his mouth drooped open, and yet none of the locusts emerged from his body.

"Is he dead? Did you kill him?"

"I don't know, what do you think?" That laugh again. It came and went ominously.

"That is what you've come to do? To bring destruction? Have others arisen?"

"You misunderstand me completely, brother Will. I am a creator." He knelt down next to Collier, and with the touch of a single finger, he burnt three squares onto the back of Collier's hand. There appeared three squares and three more squares within the first squares made.

Three sixes.

The mark of the beast.

"Now, rise," Apollyon said, and Collier's eyes flicked open. Momentarily, there was bizarre movement behind the whites of his eyes, and his former demeanor completely changed. Devoid of who he was and now possessed, he stood.

"You see?" Apollyon said to Will. "He has been given new life, when I could've so easily let him die." Apollyon laughed. "He is risen!"

"He is not alive," Will said and eyed natural paths in the woods. They split off in many different directions. He could run, get away from here, warn others.

"You're thinking of running again . . . tsk, tsk. You're very slick. I have to keep my eye on you."

Will began to pray.

"Collier," Apollyon said, and motioned toward Will.

Collier walked toward his friend. Will looked at Collier and saw that there was something missing from his eyes. His friend was gone, and there was something maniacal about him now. It resembled Apollyon's smile.

"Collier, you can fight this," Will said.

"No, he cannot."

"He can! I know how strong he is!"

"No, I have chosen one that is weak. That is what we do. We make them bend to our will, and they serve us."

Will looked at Apollyon and backed away slowly, sidestepping Collier, not giving either one of them his back.

"Remember when I said I couldn't touch you because of your faith?"

"Y . . . yes."

"It is a truth. I told you I have no reason to lie to you. You are safe from me."

Collier lashed out with blurring speed, grabbed his friend by the neck and shirt, and with great strength far beyond that any human man could possess, he manhandled Will and dragged him to the edge of the pit.

"But that doesn't mean you're safe from him. So much for friendship." Apollyon nodded. "Go ahead. Let's see if that angel knows how to fly."

Collier lifted Will and tossed his friend into the hole.

Will's cries faded as he plummeted toward the bottom. Collier tossed the cell phone in too and stood by Apollyon as if awaiting further instruction.

"No, I guess he doesn't have wings. That shouldn't surprise me. Anyhow, there isn't much time for us to accomplish what we must do before I return to the pit. Let's get going, shall we?"

CHAPTER 9

SECRETS

Sariel had tucked the book underneath his arm and walked the long journey from the "S" section to the "A," groveling the entire way. Bloody footprints stained miles of the floor throughout the Akashic Halls. Sariel retraced his steps, his feet never ceasing to bleed, his body never running out of blood.

Looking for a shortcut, he cut across new hallways, guessing a left, and looked at the names seared into the bindings. He guessed two rows back and then another left. Finally, he paused, knowing he was in the right spot. The bookcase in front of him went from floor to ceiling. Confusing as it was, he had figured out the imps' cataloging system, and the book he was looking for was in this case somewhere, among a few thousand.

This was where it got tricky because they weren't precise in their placement. He supposed as one rummaged through the shelf, chose the wrong book, and put it back, it may have been off by a book or two. But when this happened on a regular basis and for countless years, things could get quite messy.

He cricked his neck, his old eyes dimming as he tried to see up top. Everything was so faded, and some books protruded while others were pushed way back into the shelf. There was no other way.

The book case began to tremble, to shimmer without disrupting the other bookcases that were connected to it. It rocked back and forth as if someone were behind it, pushing and pulling violently. The books spilled onto the floor, falling into piles at his feet.

FWAP!

When the shelves were empty the shaking ceased, and Sariel looked at the stacks all around him. The piles were massive. His patience was worn thin.

However disorganized the shelves were before, Sariel managed to take hundreds of years' worth of work, maybe more, and in a matter of seconds, carelessly toss it to the ground. But he wasn't looking for order. Someone had clearly been hiding something from him, and he needed to find out who it was and what they knew.

The who and why ailed him more than the dysfunction and blame he'd receive from the people he used to serve—and those had been enough to drive him away from serving the dead. The damn people and their dysfunction. Maybe it would be the same thing that drove him away from his own people. They were far from perfect and quick to judge.

It was inconceivable to think someone, somehow, had come into his domain and planted these little morsels around as if it were a game. Twyla doubted him, scolded him even. Abandoned him in his time of need, and yet he knew the next clue was in the pile of books at his feet. He wished he had her there to help him sort through the mess, but the way she departed . . . things were better this way.

"She'll never see me again," he said as he knelt and rummaged through the books.

He made stacks off to the side and behind him. These were all entries he had eliminated. Surely the imps would be displeased at the mess they saw if they came this way. But he would shoo them away. He was in no mood to be interrupted or ridiculed by servants.

Although Sariel had dominion over everyone in this realm, he didn't want anyone seeing him like this. He was broken, defensive, desperate, and full of questions, doubt, paranoia, and self-destructive selfishness. It seemed as though there wasn't much difference between him and Cailean.

The need to understand who he was and why he had a strong urge to leave his duties behind outweighed everything. A tug became a pull that became a wrench from deep within that he couldn't ignore. It was so forceful that he would deceive and scheme to learn whatever it was he needed to do. He would shun those closest to him. He would break rules and not care either. God only knows what else he'd be willing to do.

Maybe if this Book of Apollyon existed, it would provide him with some answers, put him at ease. Yet, somehow, he didn't believe this would be the end of the search.

Something big was going on, and he wasn't sure what it was. It involved him, Cailean, and this being called Apollyon. Though he'd largely put Cailean and the duties of her station behind him, he only recalled her now because Twyla kept warning him about his decisions. How he wasn't allowed to do what he did.

"To hell with her and to hell with this Apollyon," he said, oddly enough, sitting in one version of hell out of the many he had created.

But those other places were of no importance to him right now.

He took hold of a leather-bound book. As old and frail as his, it crumbled beneath his touch. The cover had nearly torn off in its descent to the ground, the other heavier volumes falling on top of it.

Apollyon.

Seared into the cover, like his own name. Sariel's decrepit fingers brushed across the impression. The work from the same hand made this book, too. The fonts were identical. The sear was the same temperature, applied to the leather for the same amount of time, and with the same amount of pressure.

This was craftsmanship to be acknowledged.

Sariel wasted no time. He flipped through the pages quickly. Although this book wasn't very thick, it was filled with words, and that motivated him. He clutched both books close to his chest, and as quickly as he could he stood and moved toward the fissure. He would go to a private place to read the Book of Apollyon and see how it applied to him. He had the perfect place in mind—a place no one knew about.

Sariel had avoided the hordes of people and their Sins chasing them throughout the Valley. The stampedes were violent and never ending. People crashed through the foliage and tumbled down embankments, the mob close behind, forcing them toward their predetermined cabins so they could be judged and then get their turn. The after-judgment was the worst part, Sariel knew.

There was no other option but to run when you arrived here. It was a natural instinct to flee and try to get away.

Sariel moved farther and farther away from these chases, till the screams became so distant he would have to stop and concentrate to be able to hear them.

There was this place on the outskirts of the basin, more secret than the fissure, that would make the perfect place to study the books. Although completely covered by vegetation and invisible to anyone not looking for it, the structure still stood firm, undamaged by time.

It was simply constructed, made of mere wood, but there was significant meaning put into building this cabin. Located in a private, unused portion of the Valley, it was intended to be used as a getaway. Specifically, it was a surprise meant for Twyla. Sariel was going to take Twyla here when the opportunity arose.

Perhaps he knew somewhere deep down that, when one served humanity on deadside, an opportunity for a moment alone might never present itself. Perhaps he was naïve—an outlook he shared with none of his fellow servants. To dream of something so small but wonderful simply was at odds with the duty and unendingness of deadside. There were far too many people, moral and immoral, in need of help moving on—far more than even Sariel could imagine.

A part of most people knew they had to go, to move to the other side; but another part resisted it. All they wanted to do was live. Remain on that side of life. Their wills were strong, but they were conflicted. Sometimes, the disease or tragedy wasn't enough to kick the soul from the body, which caused a condition like being caught in the birth canal, though very much aware of it and feeling every moment of pain.

All this time serving these people, and creating ways to sort them, had drained Sariel's mind. He peeled away the thick vines and exposed the door. Built to suit him, the doorway was tall, so he didn't need to bend down. He entered the simple cabin. The inside was dark and smelled of rotting woodland and moss. The foliage had invaded the inside of the cabin and had taken over the ceiling and most of the four walls completely.

It had been five thousand years or more since he'd last seen this place.

The table remained where he had placed it, in the center of the room near the fireplace. The bed was in the corner and now looked more like a planter than a mattress.

Sariel broke apart one of the chairs, tossed the wood into the fireplace and lit himself a fire. He leaned away from the flames; winced at the light they cast. Warmth meant nothing to him. He avoided it because he preferred the coldness of death and darkness, conditions to which he had grown accustomed.

This, the fire he lit, was a way to put himself into Twyla's position. A table to rest his elbows on. A fire to burn until judgment came for the damned.

He sat at the table and slowly leaned closer to the fireplace. Sariel's robe swished, pulling him away from the fire, distracting him enough that he had to move the table farther away from the dance of the flames so he didn't feel the heat. Twyla was right. This wasn't pleasant.

He ignored his discomfort and placed the books on the tabletop, carefully inspected them, and then compared them again. Over and over again. He allowed his fingers to trace the searing burn of the names on the covers. Then he pushed his book away and pulled the Book of Apollyon close. He opened to the first page.

The Book of Apollyon
Apollyon: Destroyer
Keeper of the Bottomless Pit
Hierarchy of the Angels
Data: Incomplete

Sariel peeled back his hood, and his fingers rubbed the old parchment. It was like stepping back in time. His brows pulled close, his thoughts deep into the writings. What was the meaning behind what he was reading? He turned the page and it cracked. Several pages had been torn away, and he took the time to count how many might be missing.

"Three?" Sariel said and then read the next passage to himself.

Sariel: The Fifth Angel of Apollyon
Servant of the Dead
Destroyer

Destroyer?

His eyes hung on that word. His heart felt heavy by it. It was wrong. It had to be. He didn't destroy. He aided and had done so for thousands and thousands of years without uttering a single complaint.

"Until I brought Cailean to the false light," he said. His heart beat the inside of his chest, knowing his time with her had changed him even beyond just the thought of escaping, of ceasing to serve the dead. He had become enamored by humanity and the way they lived. Both good and bad. "Has that event started a series of events that will make me a destroyer? Is that what I'm destined to become?" Sariel asked the crackling fire.

He wanted to slide back into the darkness and disappear so that what was written couldn't come to be. But he studied the page. The words had been written in an ancient form of calligraphy known as *khatt* (خط), which was later adopted into Arabic.

Although there were varying differences in the art, it was a skill Sariel had used early on and often, and not many knew how to do it.

Each dip and swirl of the pen was meticulous in its own right. Every letter a piece of art, placed with passion and precision so that not a smudge or single line was crooked or out of place. The appearance of the ancient text was as preserved as the day it was written, with the exception of the natural aging process on the parchment, but even that was slowed down immensely in this realm.

He read the short passages again, going from the first page to what was seemingly the fifth, unsure what it all meant. What did the missing pages contain? The word 'Destroyer' bothered him more than the missing pages, and he made an effort to skip over it, but it reached out to him, demanded his attention. It labeled him.

He easily acknowledged that he was the servant of the dead because he had been that since early on in his very long existence.

But the fifth angel of Apollyon?

Destroyer?

That word again.

Data incomplete?

Who was Apollyon, and who were the other four angels before him?

The author didn't know what he or she was writing. It had to be a gathering of misinformation. Misinformation was powerful enough to start wars.

Destroyer because he was Death?

He shook his head. No, that couldn't be. It made no sense.

It was his job to take lives and escort them to the bridge beneath which the River of Life and Death flowed. Or here, to the Valley. Or was there something more to it? Something he couldn't see?

He flipped to the sixth page.

Scripture. Writings and translations will confuse the people and allow them to believe Sariel is in service of Apollyon as he delivers death.
Destruction.
He makes men run in fear.
Their hearts beat faster.
But your heart will beat forever.
You will serve the dead.
You are Death.
As surely as man will die,
you will always be
Death.

Next page.

Oh, Sariel,
your feet bleed,
your body breaks over time;
so will your discipline.
Who will pay, Destroyer?
Get to your knees and ask.
Stubbornness will be the Death
of . . .

Notation:

As you read these words, you will realize you have left a hole in the order of things. Things must be mended. Something terrible has been released to try to get you back. Hopefully, you can mend the hole that is now wide open and gaping with horrible things.

What price will you have to pay?
Look to those around you
and know the cost is high.

Sariel stopped reading. The feeling the text left behind was so ominous and disturbing, he couldn't bear it. It made him shudder. He should have listened to Twyla. Undone what he did of his own volition. He shouldn't have come here.

What had he loosed upon the world? Was this hole they spoke about a literal thing? How could he find it and confront whatever terrible being had been released to restore order?

The book gave no hint. It was merely pages of riddles.

His focus had been solely on escaping his role as Death instead of continuing to embrace his destiny to maintain universal order. The importance and trust that had been bestowed upon him had been broken. All for what? A freedom he now realized he could never have.

Twyla was right. He would have to answer for what he had done, and he believed that time for reckoning was already upon him, put in motion almost six thousand years ago with this prophecy.

With that thought, he took a closer look at the writings, studying them, placing them side by side. His eyes darted back and forth. Something old but yet familiar began to surface. It was the intimate tail applied to the letter "S." It had escaped his notice at first but was so obvious now. This minute detail was so deeply meaningful, finding it in something he shouldn't have tinkered with. He had taught this author to write the once-secreted artform!

He looked again to make sure, and he had no doubt. He sat back and groaned deep in his throat. He had no difficulty identifying who had authored these pages.

He closed the book with a slam, tapped on its cover, and contemplated his findings. His cold heart continued to pound inside his chest; his hands shook, not from the ravaging his body had taken over time, but from his discovery.

He needed to leave the cabin and get some answers to the questions that grew rapidly in his mind and complicated things further. The mystery was deep, and this was not a confrontation he looked forward to. But it was a necessary showdown.

CHAPTER 10

FREE FROM BONDAGE

"I want you to look inside yourself and ask if your love is declared in the grave or your faithfulness in destruction," Keir said.

Cailean thought. Her dead eyes revealed nothing, but the wheeze of her breathing became stronger. As she searched inside herself, her struggle was obvious, deep within and complicated.

"Look at me, Cailean."

Cailean suspended her search and looked at Keir. Her robe dangled off his body. The blackness around her was deeper, darker, colder. She shivered and dressed in the clothing Keir had given to her.

"You have been sentenced to a state of perdition. Do you remember being under the light? The feeling of death all around you? The breathing on your neck to bring you fear like you've never known?"

A spark of memory came flooding into her mind. There was snow, a voice all around her that injected fear into her. Forced her into obedience. She flinched, closed her eyes, and lowered her chin, falling into herself.

"You are not designed to serve the dead."

The memories faded as quickly as they came. She struggled to recall them as they slipped away.

"I hear their calls . . . need to usher them along. It is my job. To never tire and to never stop."

"No. Your job ended the day you died. I will not allow you to continue on and live inside a lie. You've spent most of your life doing that."

She looked at him, unpeeling herself from the tangle of memories that were wrapped tightly inside her mind. Non-linear in the way she saw things; fleeting and making no sense. Like flashes of light from a fierce lightning storm.

"What are you seeing?" Keir asked. "What is eluding you?"

"A boy. I think. He's in terrible agony. Alone, afraid . . . a wheelchair. I must go get him. Help him cross."

"No!" Keir shouted.

The sudden shout startled Cailean back to the present. Keir stepped closer to her. "What you are seeing are visions of your past. A past when you were not yet dead and not quite alive. The boy you see is your son. It is as I said: He is still very much alive."

The boy screamed, and Cailean covered her ears and cowered.

"No, he can't be alive. He's hurting, and he needs my help. I have to assist him, help him move on."

Keir grabbed her hand and pulled it away from her ear. "He's already received your help, Cailean. He's fine."

She paused. "Why do you keep calling me that name?"

"Because that *is* your name. Cailean."

She shook her head. "Have you come to fool with me? Confuse me?"

"No," Keir said and backed away. He sat on the second plank of the bridge.

"Are you a demon or a shadow person?"

"No, I am neither."

"Then what?"

"I'm a servant from Heaven, and I have come here to set you free. I'm going to help you understand what happened to you and give you a chance to confront the man who did this to you."

"Why would you do that?"

"Because things aren't right. I was sent by someone else to set things right." Keir slid his foot on the dirt, and it made a gritty sound. He whispered, "Or hope they go right." He looked at her. "She needs you to know what has been done to you. You need to be freed and have a chance to have your say before you go."

"Go where?"

Keir shrugged. "Ultimately, I'm not sure, exactly. I wasn't told, and if it wasn't mentioned, I figured it wasn't important enough to pass on." He occupied a moment by running his fingers over the divots on the wooden slats where hundreds of millions of souls had crossed. The planks showed their wear. It reminded him of the table in his room back at the cabin. The carvings etched into the tabletop. "I'm hoping it is to the light, but if I'm to be honest, I doubt it."

"Me too," Cailean said. "I don't belong in the light."

"How can you say that?"

She looked around. "The darkness is where I dwell. It provides me with comfort, helps me to hide something . . . I'm not sure what . . . but sending me to the light is an impossibility."

"The mistakes you made in your life," Keir said. "That's what you're hiding from. That's what you feel safer not knowing. It seems every time I get you to remember, the memory gets interrupted and starts you back to the beginning. We have covered some of this already. Take a moment and think. Try to push past the barrier that has been erected in your mind. Just think."

A wheelchair, screams, a stuffed animal, anger, feeling dizzy, and the sensation of falling whirled in her mind and made her stagger. "What's happening to me?"

"You are starting to remember, and the spell within is trying to keep you out. He doesn't want you to remember—and went to great lengths to make sure that doesn't happen. He never thought someone would come and talk to you. Especially someone with my experience and knowledge in what he does. Twyla was smart to send me. So, I am here. I will not leave you until I know you remember everything."

"I don't like this. I need to return to my service. So many call out to me."

"No, this thing within you will continue to ail you and won't go away if simply ignored. It must be faced here and now," Keir said. "They do not call out to *you*. They call out for Death, and whoever occupies this place will hear their calling. That is now my job. It is time for you to accept this truth and leave here. Seek the man responsible for doing this to you. Exact revenge, if you wish. Whatever your decision, you don't belong here, and I will not allow you to stay."

"I—"

"You were tricked. Lied to. Used as a pawn and given no decision in what made you—" Keir studied her—"this."

"How?" Her curiosity increased in an attempt to put it all together. "How was I fooled?"

"A grand design by an angel who is in service of the dead. His name is Sariel, and he chose you to take his post."

"What . . . I mean how?"

"You don't belong here. Do you not feel unnatural? You cannot do what he has placed you here to do. You need to listen to my words, feel what's inside your body. You are vulnerable now as you were then."

Cailean looked down. Her skin was already pale from the lack of light. Her body already showing signs of wear from the road she walked.

"A human body wasn't built to withstand what he scheduled you to do. Look at what it has done to you already, and your service has just begun."

"Then tell me. What did this Sariel do?"

"He chose you. Picked you out of millions in a moment. Brought you to his perverted version of limbo and made you confront the errors in your life. You made significant mistakes, and the boy you hear . . . this has affected him, too. Sariel cruelly included him."

"That's why I hear him now?"

"No. That is but a memory. You won't remember anything after the transformation he had you undergo to become the ambassador of death—unless I show you. Force the memories back into your mind."

Cailean grabbed her head, dropped to her knees, and looked at Keir. "I'm so confused. The voices are so loud."

"Allow me to help you clear it up then. You must go and confront him. We are running out of time. He will finish the rest. Do what must be done."

Her eyes agreed to his terms.

"There was an accident, and it involved you and your son. You had fallen on him after you hit your head. You and he were dying. You from your head wounds, and him from the crushing weight of your body on his small body. You almost smothered him to death. You were given a choice. Accept this role and your son lives, or decline it and you both die."

The information was surreal, somehow distant and yet intimately angering. She rose to her feet.

"What was my son's name?"

"Not was—is. His name is Beau. I've told you these things already."

"Beau," she whispered and smiled for the first time since she'd put on the mantle of death. "I like that name." She paused. "The things you tell me are hard to retain."

"I know. Excuse my frustration. Beau has turned out to be a fine young man. He's developed . . . gifts."

"What sort of gifts?"

"Gifts for the better. He helps those in need." Keir hesitated. "I give you the truth. Sariel intended on keeping you here forever while he roamed free from the promise he made to serve the dead. He did this to seek things he shouldn't."

"So, I can leave?"

"You can do whatever you wish, except stay here."

"How could he be so cruel?"

"It is in his nature. He's a destroyer of life, hope, and trust. I'm afraid, after he had dealings with you, it has only worsened. He wasn't like this before. He was kind, caring, and had a genuine love for the people. That was in the beginning. But as all things age and tire, they change. In his case, he's been tainted . . . soured somehow."

"Where can I find him, this Sariel?"

Keir stood. "He thinks he's the only one who knows, but I know exactly where he is. You must hurry because he intends on leaving, and you must intercept him before he does. I am a keeper, and it is my job to know all these things."

"Who will care for the dead when I leave?"

"Remember, I said that is my job now. At least for the time being."

"But you are just a child."

"No, Cailean, I am much more than a child and so much older than you could ever imagine."

"Where can I find him?"

"There is a place in the Valley where you send the sinful. You can find him there, on the outskirts. He is close. Let me explain to you how you're going to get there from here."

Keir ran his fingers through the dirt and drew a simple map. He asked her to repeat what he told her, and when she did, he stood, satisfied.

"Now go, and no matter what happens, don't ever come back here again."

Cailean fled into the darkness as Keir adjusted the oversized robe, covered his head with the hood, and ventured to the calling voices.

CHAPTER 11

THE CABIN

Twyla shook her head, slid into the seat in the center of the room, and rested her elbows on the table. A certain nervousness followed her around, taking up the seat right next to her. It wanted to hold hands, get close, but she ignored it. It had no place here. She believed that whatever happened here was what was meant to happen. Nerves, worry, and the inevitable were on a collision course, and she was right at their intersection.

In the fireplace, the burning logs popped and threw embers up the chimney. Besides that, the cabin felt empty; Keir had cleaned the room before he'd departed upon her request. An eerie silence settled around her. There was no book in front of her to study as she waited for the next sinner. An odd feeling; she briefly felt as though she were skirting her responsibilities as Sariel had. But she knew better. Being here, facing what was to come, proved her dedication.

Even though Keir was quiet, always encapsulated in his thoughts on what needed to be done next, it had been nice having him around. Though the company had grown more and more silent as the years passed, Keir was good to her, looked after her, and knew how to handle the people. He had defused countless confrontations—even the most troubled and volatile, like Leopold Conroy. Because of that, she knew she was the luckiest keeper in the entire Valley.

This was the first time since Keir was assigned to her that he had ventured out of the shelter of their shanty. It was necessary to send him, though, because Sariel was becoming everything she feared.

Reckless.

Angry.

A stranger.

Unstoppable in his quest for answers, an urge that seemingly came from nowhere. But she knew where it had manifested from: the people and their sinful ways. The sheer amount of people they couldn't have possibly perceived when they took on this role. The blame, feeling of rejection, and the need to escape it had pushed him away and over an invisible edge.

Sariel had created a dangerous rift with his actions, and that meant sacrifices must be made, wrongs righted; a new chapter would begin. Roles would be recast. A change of guard of sorts.

No, that wasn't right.

"Ahh," she grumbled, unable to get her mind to focus because of those damn nerves. But she knew what she meant.

She pressed her hands into her face, rubbed the skin as if to flatten out the wrinkles. This moment had been foretold, and she had prepared herself for it, but she never thought it would come so soon. Sariel was special in every way. Caring. Compassionate. A leader. A true visionary.

But, she supposed, it had always been a matter of when. *When* had come, and she wasn't prepared. She reflected: No matter how many years passed, she didn't think she would ever be ready for this. But yet here it was, happening all too quickly.

Staring at the fire, ignoring that nagging she felt sitting beside her, she wondered: How long until Sariel started to figure things out?

She wondered if he would come to help her and if it was even possible for him to stop this. She supposed not, but it didn't hurt to hold onto hope.

But, she supposed, it didn't matter because soon there would be a knock on the door. A knock that was foretold five-thousand five-hundred years ago. She had been told by the one who had met with her in the catacombs back when they were being newly constructed. That was the first and only time she had met that woman. She was pleasant and certain in everything she said. But she promised Twyla the tribulation period would end, though not until after the suffering. All to give new purpose. To refocus what had become blurry.

There was no denying that fear entered Twyla's heart now. Fear could be an amazing motivator. She had told that to the sinful countless times. Now she understood how true her words were and found them quite discomforting. Like bugs that crawled beneath your skin.

She stood and watched the flames for a bit more, hoping to harness the destructive force of the blaze. Leo had said it was mesmerizing how when he held his hands out to feel the heat that it provided him comfort. She needed its anger, the rage that ravaged the wood and devoured whatever was in its path and nothing else.

Her compassionate side needed to fall away in a pile of ash, her connection to beautiful things, just like Sariel had, needed to die if she wanted to endure what was to come. Overcome by emotion that she had been put into this situation by someone who was supposed to love her, Twyla bit down and clenched her fists.

Why wouldn't you listen to me?

But bad decisions always required a price to be paid. A debt owed that must be fulfilled to create balance. There was counterbalance in everything because that was the way the world was made. The yin and the yang. Male and female. Hot and cold. Life and Death. The analogies went on and on, proving that balance ruled the universe.

There were no regrets in what she had to do now, or then. It was the order; the command that must be obeyed. Unlike Sariel, she couldn't ignore it no matter how much she wanted to. Denial, desperation, and ultimately accepting that her fate was unchangeable, she allowed her hands to relax and uncurl.

This was the only way to usher the change that needed to take place in order for him to come back. This moment was an act of love *for* him.

Tap, tap, tap.

Her heart skipped a beat, and she looked at the door. They had come. The anger inside no longer burned; rather, the pang of nerves shook her.

She had faced evil so many times, countered it without injury, so these nerves felt out of place. A distraction from her impending destiny. But all of the evil she'd encountered was just practice, readying her for the most malevolent thing she would ever face. She opened the door, turned her back, and returned to her seat.

Apollyon entered the cabin with a man in tow. The man who followed the demon had distant eyes, and there was unusual movement in the whites.

"You turn your back to me and sit?" Apollyon said. He chuckled. "I have come from the abyss. Freed to come and take you deep down into the earth to make Sariel suffer."

"I know where you come from, who you are, and what you intend to do. Am I to fear you? Bow down and just go with you?"

Apollyon looked around the cabin. "I don't know, should you? You operate on feeling—what your gut tells you based on some pictures conceived long before the person ever was—don't you? I know you normally have books to help you, but I don't see the book in front of you. Did someone else take it?"

"There's nothing in there that would help me or you in this situation. We are natural enemies. The outcome will be determined by how we proceed in handling our differences. Knowing that there may be no resolve but physical violence, I still invited you into my home."

"I could have huffed and puffed if you did not."

Twyla smirked and with it, a laugh escaped.

"You laugh when you know what the outcome is going to be?" Apollyon said, his confidence strong.

"I laugh at the look of you. That your kind was once beautiful but has been turned into something grotesque because you choose to do wrong."

"In whose eyes?" Apollyon shrugged. "Certainly not mine. I didn't come here expecting you to cower before me. I know what hides underneath that old skin suit you wear."

"Informed while sealed in a pocket deep down where the earth boils?"

Apollyon looked at his companion. "Have a seat, Collier, and then look at her. Watch what is to happen. Bear witness. Be the messenger that speaks to Death when he comes."

Collier sat and stared.

"You'd be surprised how resourceful we can be in getting messages around. Like you, we don't intend on going down without a fight. We plan, work together, expect what is to come but prepare, knowing if we stand together, the outcome we seek is achievable."

"I think you are dreaming. You and everyone like you."

"We won't lose."

Twyla enjoyed another laugh but sensed things were turning serious now. "So confident." She knew what was about to happen and braced herself. "One little victory here and there has given your kind a false sense of hope. It has lulled all of you into thinking you can change what will be."

"Let's not go in circles here, Twyla. You know what I've come to do. You know what you must do, too."

Twyla stood. "I do," she said. A glowing light surrounded her and began to scorch, burning brightly though not actually hot.

Apollyon half-circled the table. "I won't hide that I have relished this opportunity now that it's come. A chance to see topside, breathe fresh air not tainted by brimstone. The shouts have faded from my ears, and it is a good reprieve. But they will begin again soon. You will scream. Ah, I do regret having to return to the pit though. But, I know it must be. And at least it will be with some company."

Twyla glanced at the darkened doorway that led to the Akashic Halls. There was no sign of Sariel. She felt her heart sink, swallowed hard, and faced Apollyon. "You speak of a bounty you haven't yet collected. Enough talk. We both know what must happen here, so let's get this over with, shall we?"

"He's not coming to save you. He's lost," Apollyon said and then bowed. Not out of respect, but as a sign that he was ready for battle. With that signal, Twyla underwent a quick transformation. Her old, decrepit body reconstructed into something heavenly. Her youth returned, beauty bound from the cast of Heaven, and white, majestic wings flapped open. A beaming light formed in her right fist, and a sword grew from the light.

Apollyon changed too. The skin on his face pulled tight; bone protruded and formed into sharp spikes. His body began to glow; the red fire he controlled bubbled to the surface of his skin. Flaming flesh distorted the air around him like heat from blacktop. It collided with the cool cabin air. Then, lastly, wings snapped out from behind his back, the span far greater than Twyla's, and the feathers black like that of a raven.

The wingspan showed status and strength.

In tandem, the two took flight and collided in midair. Twyla swung her sword. Apollyon, clearly much stronger, grabbed Twyla by the arms and easily defended her attack. He pumped his wings and slammed her into the wooden wall, and it splintered. Feathers rained down like confetti, and grunts filled the room as the initial struggle began.

Crashing a fist into Twyla's cheek and following up with a headbutt, Apollyon held her against the wall, suspending her from a fall, her body cradled in the indent, his forearm across her throat as she choked. Lightheadedness took over as his spikes sliced her skin and she bled.

Her thoughts were confused; her head rang from the blow it absorbed, and she knew she was in trouble. Terrible trouble.

"Father?"

Desensitized and running on adrenaline and survival instincts, she felt the need to prevail over her natural enemy. Thankfully, she didn't feel the burn of his touch. Twyla pushed back with an animalistic growl and shoved Apollyon, creating a small space between them.

"Is not coming for you either," Apollyon mocked.

Controlling the sword with her mind, she shrunk it in her fist and turned it into a dagger. She used every effort to jab it into Apollyon's belly, and it sunk in deep. She twisted the handle and snapped the light off inside his body.

His eyes widened, and he fell to the ground, knocking over the table and empty chair, just missing Collier.

Her work here was done.

He rolled, hissed as he grabbed at the area where the handle of the dagger should have been.

"You!" he shouted and pointed. "You dare desecrate my body with your filthy light!"

He saw the shimmering light dull and burn out beneath his flesh. He heated his fist and cauterized the wound.

Twyla landed on the ground and looked at him with a smile of victory. She took the handle of the dagger and tossed it into the fire. The flames glowed, and Apollyon puffed his chest and expanded his wings.

"Now they can track you. You are vain, Apollyon. It was wonderful doing battle with you. To show you that you are not untouchable."

"You dare taint me?"

"You dare taint us by trespassing on our land?"

"I was going to take it easy on you, but now you've disfigured me with the light from above. Marked me as if I were cattle to be branded."

Apollyon slammed into Twyla again, and both bared clenched teeth as they wrestled for control over the other. Punches from each side landed, some just glancing blows and others devastating powerhouses meant to maim and incapacitate.

"You will—"

Apollyon swiped his fingernails across her cheek. Three bleeding lines that would scar her forever burned her skin. He took advantage of her setback and bear-hugged her. His massive wings enveloped her, wrapped tightly as they squeezed like a snake that once slithered in a perfect Garden. A Garden she wished she were still in with Sariel before all this madness came to be.

Apollyon looked into her eyes, mocking everything that she believed. The pressure he applied forced tears from her eyes, but she remained defiant to his power and tried to resist.

A hand slid around her side and to her back. It grabbed hold of the backbone where the right wing connected to her body. Apollyon pulled down with great force and slowly separated the bone from skin and cartilage.

As the bone broke and cartilage tore, Twyla tried to shout out in pain but had no air to do so. She couldn't move. Couldn't wail. Couldn't do anything about what was happening to her, and her thoughts moved to Sariel. She hoped he would become what he was supposed to be. That Keir would be successful in delivering that message.

With a loud snap, Apollyon had torn the wing off her body. The glow of the fireplace began to dim. Her need to fight left along with the oxygen she required to remain conscious.

She went limp.

As quickly as it had started, it was over. Apollyon opened his wings, and Twyla collapsed to the floor with a heavy thump. He righted the table and laid the torn, bloodied wing on it, then patted Collier on the head.

"Remember everything you saw here."

He returned to Twyla. "Now for the other one."

Apollyon ripped the other wing off her body and placed that on the table, too. Blood covered the floor, walls, and ceiling.

"Make sure you tell him what was done here. Listen to the things I put inside you."

Just then, Asmodeus walked into the cabin and looked at Apollyon, taking notice of his injury, then of the destruction.

"It is nothing," Apollyon said and turned his body away in an attempt to hide the wound. "I have sealed it and have plenty of time to address it."

"Very good," he said. "Do with her what you will. Our deal is finished. You have your prize. Now, do the honorable thing and return where I released you from."

"I intend to. At least for the time being I will have someone to occupy my time. I'll question her, make her beg for the torment to stop."

"I would do so much more."

"I am not you," Apollyon said. "Besides, there is plenty of time for me to decide what else I'm going to do with her."

"No, you certainly are not me. That doesn't need to be defended by either one of us. Now, go. A deal is a deal. Once you descend into your pit, it will be sealed again."

Apollyon sniffed Twyla. "Gladly." He lifted her body and slung her over his shoulder.

Asmodeus tilted his hat as a gesture of respect, turned, and walked into a room at the end of the hallway. He left the door open a crack.

Apollyon exited the cabin with Twyla, and Collier remained behind. The undead man's eyes were focused on the white wings with the bloody stumps that dripped at the end.

Something that was once beautiful was now tragic in every way, and the things inside him buzzed around with excitement, eager to tell of the things they'd witnessed.

CHAPTER 12

CONFRONTATION

The fire had been extinguished, smothered by the cloak. The smoldering wood belched wispy gray smoke into the chimney. It reminded him of the ashen human soul, so lost and afraid as it slid from the physical vessel to its new body on this side. Although still in form, it was shadowy, transparent, like the smoke. Sometimes new souls on this side were as helpless as newborn children.

Sariel fell out of his reverie, tucked the books beneath his arm, and exited the cabin. He took a moment to close the door behind himself and make sure it was sealed. Unable to ignore his shock at why Twyla had written the books and never told him, he remained distracted. Her involvement in all of this was so confusing . . . angering even. Did he really know who she was?

She had kept the secret from him and never hinted at it. He wondered if it ate her up inside to betray her long-ago lover and supposed best friend. Or was it easy to do? A task like taking in one of the sinful—setting them up, and then sending them along to their judgement?

He pressed his hands against the door, rested his head, smelled the old leather.

"I will always be alone," he said. "Who would want something like me? Broken and disgusting in every way. Unlovable."

He gathered himself, tucked his broken heart away, and turned to venture through the forest. Twyla's cabin was where he needed to be next. He hoped he would gain some insight, find some answers—and then cut off their friendship forever. The questions he needed to ask weren't complicated: Why? Why wouldn't you *tell* me, Twyla? And what does all of this mean?

Suddenly, something broke through the foliage, raced toward him, and slammed into him with such force it made him lose his grip on the books and knocked him backward.

Sariel felt his bones crack as he collided with the side of the cabin. A barrage of punches and kicks kept him off balance and hardly able to defend himself. His sense of understanding was lost somewhere in the stars that filled his head.

He could do away with his attacker with the power of his mind, a wave of his hand, or a flick of his finger if he weren't so lost within himself. He felt the anger in the assault, tried to imagine who it might be, but the constant ceaseless attack kept him much too busy to settle on an answer.

After the initial blows, and with the element of surprise taken away, the intensity lessened to the point where he could look to see who it was that had come for him.

"You son of a bitch!"

He looked into Cailean's eyes. Her face filled with rage, her fists clenched, and she bared her teeth. She paused as she glared back at him. Her eyes burned with scorn; his with surprise and regret.

She remained above him, huffing, her eyes as wide as they could be, the anger she exuded tangible and urgent.

"If I didn't tire out I would've finished what I started."

Sariel stood, using the wall to help him get his feet beneath him. He didn't take his eyes off of her. Her attack was brutal, and he could feel the physical effects of it. His forearms stung from trying to shield his vulnerable areas. His head and even his legs were sore from the attack.

"I deserved that," Sariel said. "But I won't pretend how curious I am to know how you found me here."

"I was told what you did to me and to my son!"

"I saved your son. You should be thankful, not angry!"

"You put us through hell is what you did!"

"I saved you from yourself. I saved your son from you. Hang onto your anger. Anything you've done in your short lifespan has been far worse than anything I've done since the beginning."

Cailean swung at him, but this time he shrugged away her blow. "You don't even have remorse for the things you've done to me!"

"No," Sariel said. "I don't and never will. You can search for it from here to eternity, and I will never feel bad for you. I've never seen anyone more deserving of what she got than you."

"How could you?"

"I asked you the same thing and your answers were pitiful, just like your accusations are right now. But like I said, I have no pity for you."

"What sort of monster are you?" Cailean asked, her anger giving way to emotions she'd buried till now.

"I am the meaning and the end."

"What . . . " She tilted her head and seemed to forget her anger for the moment. "What is that supposed to mean?"

"That I am Death, and without me, life would have no meaning. But in the end, the one that gives your life meaning takes it away."

"That's a shame," Cailean said. "Knowing you are the last thing people ever see."

Sariel laughed. "There are things far worse than me. I'm looking at one right now. And I am not the last they see."

Cailean blinked her red, wet eyes.

"I can show you, if you wish to remember."

"No, I know what I was, just like I know what you are. I've seen enough."

A howl far off in the distance made her sniff back her tears. She turned her head toward the sound.

"They're wild," Sariel said. "They're coming for you. You're right to back away, and you should be concerned by their coming."

Cailean backed up to Sariel. The forest was so thick she couldn't see a thing. The throaty noises continued, and the branches moved as the things continued to maneuver around. "A rabid animal?"

"Something like that. Now do you know what I'm talking about? I'm not so bad now, am I? The real monsters are coming, and they're coming for you!"

Cailean didn't respond. Her eyes followed the sounds of sticks snapping underfoot. Suddenly, they seemed to be all around, having managed to encircle her.

"Go ahead, scream, let her know you are here," Sariel said in a loud voice. "Scream, Sins!"

The howls were loud and close, seemingly within reach now. Cailean found herself moving closer to Sariel for protection, even grabbing his cloak.

"So, who told you the things you know? Who told you how to find me?"

"What does that matter right now?"

"It matters so much that words can't express it. You telling me is the difference between being with me, or them. Choose your monster."

Cailean whined.

"I'm the only one who can protect you here. Being in the Valley exposes you to your Sins. Parts of you were left here, waiting for you to die. The things around us are what you were destined to face. To fear what you've created for all eternity. But I kept you from that, and you come at me with anger, violence, and accusations about my character?" He looked out into the brush. "I should just leave you here." Sariel shoved her away. "If you believe what you said, I want you to go. Run as fast as you can, and don't you ever stop, because they won't."

"Stop!" True fright echoed in her shout. "How do I know this isn't some sort of setup?"

"You don't. You can go—I won't stop you. Or you can tell me who sent you, and I will protect you."

Cailean's eyes were wide as they scanned the foliage. "A boy. He said his name was Keir."

"Keir?" Sariel replied in surprise. He embraced the many scenarios in his mind. "I wonder what he has to do with this."

"I don't know. But he told me everything you did to me, made me understand when I didn't want to, and said someone had sent him. That I needed to be here."

"Oh no," Sariel said. His face turned to stone, his heart colder than ice. "Did he tell you who had sent him?"

"A woman. I don't remember her name. It was odd. Unique."

In that instant, Sariel knew. "Twyla," he uttered between gritted teeth. She must have been commissioned to restore his role. That was why they were put together early on. It was a way to watch over him. Control him, if need be.

"Twyla," Sariel whispered again and paced. "How could she?"

"Yes, that's it!"

"What?" Sariel said and snapped out of his trance.

"That was her name."

"But why?" Sariel dropped to his knees and looked down at the ground. Everything he'd known about himself and those who were assigned to serve with him was a lie. "No!" he shouted and pounded his fist into the soil.

Just then, one of Cailean's Sins stepped out from behind the cover of plant life, watching her with uneven eyes. It growled with a deformed mouth and dislocated jaw that revealed several missing teeth. It lunged at her, and Sariel seemed to forget his pain. He stood tall and caught it in midair by the throat. It dangled in his grasp, flopping as it tried to escape the unbreakable hold.

Startled, Cailean shouted out, "What the hell is that?"

"The Sins of your life that have come to get you, and they have come at a time that will be their undoing!"

Sariel tossed the thing aside, and three more tried to get to her. Sariel swung around, batting them away with ease. It seemed the anger brought out by a betrayed heart tapped into his power, which he'd reserved till now.

Another wave of attacks came, and there had to be at least ten this time. Again, he moved quickly to dispatch them. But more were advancing, coming quicker now, more frequently.

"Remember when I said you could run and never stop?"

"Yes."

"You must go! There are too many of them for me to keep you safe."

"But I told you who sent me. You said you would protect me."

"And that was what my intentions were." He tossed another aside, knocking several over in the process. "When I originally took you, I knew how bad a person you were. But seeing this . . ."

He picked her up, showing her the crowd that came for her. There had to be hundreds, maybe even thousands. They went on as far as the eyes could see. He put her down.

"Now do you see how bad you really were? Do you understand that I saved you from a hellish fate? Do you wish to face them or opt out? You must decide now."

"I want out."

"Then I want you to remember that what I'm about to do is an act of mercy. It's an apology for what I have done to you, and it is the only way out for you." Sariel darted forward, grabbed Cailean by her neck, and picked her up so that her feet dangled. He twisted his wrist and snapped her neck. Her body went limp, but he didn't let her go. He held her up high for her Sins to see, and they all howled out in anguish. Some fell to their knees, pounding the ground, while others began to fight with each other.

Sariel picked up his books, carried Cailean's body into the secreted cabin, locked the door behind himself, and rested her corpse on the mattress.

"What have I done?" he said as he knelt over her pale, lifeless body. He brushed her eyes closed and sat in distress and regret. "Twyla, why have you forsaken me?"

The Sins pounded on the door.

He had killed a human, not ushered one along. Although it was intended to be a mercy killing, it was as much a desperate cover-up for what he had done. To set her free in the wilderness would be reckless. He had no idea how her time as Death had changed her. What powers might she have gained?

Thoom!

The things outside crashed into the door. He looked toward the sound and wondered how he would pacify her Sins. He had taken their purpose away, and they would never be satisfied. They would claw and pull at the cabin until they breached it and got to her. But what would they do when they found she couldn't run and they couldn't chase?

Never had this happened before. And although these were all very serious concerns, they would have to wait. He stood, his mind shifting to his need to get to Twyla's cabin and confront her.

Discovering she had written these books, having sent Keir to inform Cailean about what he'd done, and assigning him take Sariel's post as Death were all very disconcerting.

He'd found that the further he dug, the more problems and questions he created. Although Sariel increasingly had bouts of anger, what was rising within him now was something so strong, so consuming, that if unleashed, there would be mass destruction in his wake. He closed his eyes and saw the words in his mind: *Sariel: Destroyer.*

CHAPTER 13

DEATH IS A CHILD

The muscle car had flipped upside down after broadsiding a limousine. The streets were littered with debris, and a shocked, growing crowd of on-lookers gathered on the sidewalk. Cries came from inside the limo, and another screamed from the flipped car. The occupant called out for help. He was in a state of shock and panic. Keir went to him first. The man saw Keir from within the twisted wreckage and reached out to take the young boy's hand.

"Help me, please," he said.

Keir could smell the alcohol, and it saddened him. This all could have been avoided with a better decision. The single male occupant inside was covered in blood, pinned behind the steering wheel, broken bones throughout his body, his consciousness fading in and out.

"Please . . ."

Thoughts of his life, friends, and family sped through his mind, and Keir could see them all. What would they think of him when they found out what he had done? His fat, bloody lips mumbled their names. First his mother, then his father, then a little sister, and big brother who had started a family of his own. This could have happened to them if they crossed paths with someone like him.

It had been a foolish decision to drink and drive, and the man knew it. He had caused this. He shouldn't have listened to the voice inside his head that told him to take the keys, leave the bar, and go. He could barely get the key into the ignition.

The voice wanted him to test the muscle car, push it to its limits. His impairment had taken away his better judgment, and instead he'd wanted to feel the exhilaration of controlling the vehicle as it sped through traffic. The engine had responded with a growl, eager to show its speed. Now it had cost him a debt he had no idea how to repay.

Keir, enrobed in black, watched the young man. His soul was in such distress that Keir could hardly stand seeing it trapped like that.

The boy assessed the situation, looked deep into the young man's soul, and knew where he had to take him. This was the shameful part of humanity, and it was the first of that kind he'd had to serve since taking the robe.

Keir reached forward, grabbed the man by his hand, and pulled. His physical body went limp; the last breath leaked out of his lungs, and he tipped, leaning against shattered glass and twisted metal. It would take the jaws of life to remove his corpse.

"Come with me, mister," Keir said. "We need to go for a walk that will take us far away from here."

"My name is Tyler."

"I know your name. That doesn't make much of a difference to me. What you did . . ." Keir shook his head.

The man sank into a deep state of confusion and looked at the wreckage. It was chaos tied into a metallic knot. He looked at the boy with the same disorientation.

"What happened?"

"You've died," Keir said. "You've been in a car accident, and it has killed you. Drunk driving. Your time here has come to an end, and I am to escort you. Do you understand that?"

"Escort me where?"

"Where we are now is where the agent of Death operates. Humans don't remain here. It is but a place of transition to the other side."

"And you . . . you're Death?"

Keir squeezed the man's hand and gave it a tug. "Come, we must go. There is nothing left for you on that side. You've hurt people, created a bad situation that will be long lasting for someone. It has only made someone who should've been inconspicuous more brazen. But it is done and cannot be undone, so let us not dwell. You're destined to move on now."

"I'm sorry."

"Don't say sorry to me, mister. It's the people you have changed forevermore you should be sorry to. The woman in the vehicle you hit will have to live with what happened this day. The trials she will have to go through are unthinkable, and you get a pass by my pulling you from that wreckage. Everyone is always sorry after the fact. Sorry fixes nothing when foolishness prevails. If you could see the destruction, the wake of pain you've left behind, you would know 'sorry' has little meaning."

Tyler wallowed in that accusation. "Somehow, I know that to be true."

"Come, I must move you on. Like I said, let us not dwell. There are others in need."

"But, you're just a child."

"Who were you expecting?" Keir mused. "A man with a skull face wielding a scythe?"

Tyler followed Keir without resistance and remained quiet.

"Don't you find my presence so much more endearing? Less frightening?"

"Yes," Tyler said. "Yes, of course. But this goes— *you* go against everything we believe about death and what it is like."

"There are others who roam that side of existence and manipulate things on purpose to keep people confused and far away from the truth."

"Why? Why is it like that?"

Keir shrugged. "Spiritual warfare is a complicated thing, mister. It has been going on for a long time, and I couldn't get you to understand a fraction of it by the time we reach our destination."

"How do I get in? Are there gates?"

"No, no gates for you. There's just the forest. That's where you'll be going. I'll take you there, and you will need to find your destination on your own."

"How will I know where to go?"

"As your lungs knew to pull in air and your heart knew to beat, you will know."

"OK," he said and followed Keir.

They walked in silence across the flat land. The dark was so deep it kept everything a secret.

"Who is Sariel?" Tyler asked, the question more of an afterthought.

Keir stopped. "Where did you hear that name?"

"I don't know. From the same voice that told me I was sober enough to drive. That I should drive fast and that I could make it across the intersection in time before the light changed."

"It is curious you would say that name."

"Why?"

"You weren't alone."

"I was alone. I've always been a loner."

"Not with friends, but in here." Keir tapped his temple and his heart. "Sariel is Death."

"Where is he?"

"He's lost, like you, and needs to find his way back home."

"Home is here?"

"Yes. For him, not you."

"There was a part of me that was desperate to get away before Sariel came. But not *me* . . . I had a curiosity about me, planted there somehow. Does that make sense?"

"Yes, I think so," Keir said.

"It said that it, this part of me, needed to go before Sariel came. Whatever that was, that feeling, it didn't want to see him or him to see it."

"I know who you speak of," Keir said. "It seems things are much more complicated than I originally thought."

Keir and Tyler came upon the Great Divide, and the distant moonlight lit up the thick forest.

"When you step across the divide, you must run. That is what your mind will tell you, and you will instinctively obey. You will run fast, and the path you will be on will be treacherous and will test your will . . . to see how much you want to continue to exist."

"Where am I running to?"

"Your new life."

Keir nudged Tyler into the forest. As Keir had said, Tyler began to run and let out a scream as he picked up speed. Curious about Tyler's words, Keir was certain the man had either been influenced or possessed on the other side by a demon who feared Sariel.

"Sardurvial," Keir whispered. He sensed spiritual warfare on the horizon—it was deepening far beyond anything the likes of which he had seen in the past. Although word of Sariel's parting might not have spread that far, strangely enough, the influencers on the other side seemed to be more and more active. Keir turned away. "At least Sariel's temporary parting might have been contained by Twyla," he muttered to himself. "Maybe these things that have happened will get him back into place in time to restore order."

With a troubled heart, Keir headed back for the man in the limousine. A newlywed, the young groom would never see his new bride again. That good man, a poor soul who'd had the misfortune of crossing paths with a drunk driver on his wedding day, needed to be escorted to the bridge.

CHAPTER 14

A DEAL SEALED

Apollyon carried Twyla's limp, bleeding body to the pit he'd emerged from. Her face was so swollen that one eye was completely closed. The two massive, hollow crevices on her back oozed from deep within. Her angelic appearance had been beaten down into something that looked subhuman.

Apollyon looked down into the deep, dark hole and felt the simmering heat exuding from the depths. As much as he liked topside, he missed what was below. He had grown accustomed to the heat and the company of those who had been bound there with him. They were his kin, and he was glad to know he had them to go to war with. Though he'd never admit it, he even kind of missed the stink of the old place.

A squawk from a nearby tree drew his attention, and he located the hawk. It spread its tail feathers out in the shape of a V, flapped its wings, held them out wide, bobbed its head as it ran back and forth on the branch, and squawked one last time before it leapt. Gliding through the air, the bird flew away to deliver its message.

The remaining locusts buzzed, still clamoring for position on the tree they'd attached themselves to.

"The two strongest, I want you to go now," Apollyon said. This part of his plan was not agreed upon when Asmodeus freed him. The locusts had been released merely as protection, but they served a greater purpose. It would be wise of him to keep a few brokers topside. Surely, they would come in handy one day. "Choose and do your work. Now go! You know what to do!"

Two flew away, both taking to the same direction, while the others persisted in their endless dance for dominance over each other. Dead locusts had accumulated at the base of the tree, having been overcome by the struggle. The dance would continue until all were dead.

Apollyon opened his wings part of the way, curved them outward so they made a U-shape, and pushed them downward, allowing him to glide in a straight descent.

He jumped, his fall slowed by his wings, the wind strong enough to pull out loose feathers and strain the muscles and tendons he relied on for control. The added weight of having to carry Twyla created extra pressure, and the force of air rushing upward created uncalculated wind resistance. Apollyon strategically worked the air with his wings as he neared the bottom of the pit, coming dangerously close to the jagged walls a few times.

Apollyon's feet touched down on the blazing hot stone floor. He'd landed next to the red-stained shape of a man on the ground. The man's remains were long gone, mashed into small pieces of meat and bone that had fed those who were still chained.

Apollyon spun around the room with Twyla's limp, bleeding body, holding her up high for all to see.

The fallen who had been left behind and chained to the walls all watched, astonished at Apollyon's spoils. He laid Twyla down on the middle of the hardened ground of the tomb they had been sealed in and would be sealed in once more.

"She is ours to keep," Apollyon said, now a champion to those who were still bound. "This is why I went. A gift from Asmodeus for risking myself by going topside and entering the Valley to make Death pay for killing one of our own. I have taken his favorite, hurt him to his core, and now she is ours. Hidden away. Our toy."

"Sariel will come," one of the bound said, afraid.

"Let him come. He is weaker away from dead-side," Apollyon said. "I don't fear him, and neither should you."

Apollyon's flesh began to redden, and Twyla's blistered. The blood that oozed from her back bubbled and started to crust over.

"Imagine the torment," Apollyon said as he encircled Twyla. "Imagine how long we can keep her here to do as we wish."

"Is she—"

Apollyon raised a finger. "Not to be touched by anyone, but rather, tormented as much as you want. Think of her as a plaything. I've incapacitated her, so I know she won't get away. Her wings are gone." He knelt. "Her precious wings. So white and pure, tainted with the stain of red." He stood and looked at everyone around him. "I've left them behind to show Sariel that we are still around. Not to be forgotten, and not to be messed with. It is a gift of sorts . . . a reminder of her torment. To see his face when he discovers she is here would be glorious, but, alas, it is not meant for me to see."

"Her wings—that will incense him!" someone said appreciatively.

"Yes!" Apollyon said. "Our day is drawing near. Once I get the key and free you all, you can do what you will to her and the people. Do we fear Sariel then? Just like when a natural disaster hits, he will be so busy he won't have time to deal with us."

"What was it like up there?"

"Breathtaking. The world is beautiful, and the people don't deserve it. They don't appreciate it. But, we know this, don't we? That is why we have been cast aside."

"Yes," the group said in unison. "We have been cast down for them."

"Because of them," Apollyon said. "One day it will be ours."

Apollyon dragged Twyla's limp body over to an unoccupied outcropping of rock and limestone next to the crack that freed him. Shackles that once bound him he now placed on her wrists, ankles, and neck. He worked tirelessly to make sure the chains and once-broken shackles were fixed and unbreakable. Using all of his might to secure the anchors into the wall, he created a binding that could not be undone.

"They will come," Twyla managed to say.

"You have awakened, my dear tortured angel?"

"And when they do, they will kill you all for what you have done. Everyone here will be dead because of you. You do not stand a chance."

"None of us are afraid, sweet Twyla. We welcome our chance to prove our worth against the immortal Sariel. The keeper of the dead. The poor, broken servant." Apollyon spun on his heels. "Some say we have seven years to rule the earth."

Twyla spat blood and groaned. "That is merely a speck of time in the grander picture of what is to come. Those unfortunate enough to still be alive will occupy these heated caverns for eternity. This place will soon be filled with molten lava, and you lot will have no chance of ever escaping. That is, if Sariel allows you to live. And I have a feeling the 'if' is slim."

Apollyon knelt in front of Twyla, took her chin, guided her face up to his. "And you will remain right here, chained to this wall to experience that with us. There is no escape for you. Imagine the pain as your lungs fill with molten earth. There is only torment now. No one knows where you are." He narrowed his focus. "And if he were to come to kill me as you say, I will kill you first, and I will make sure he sees it, too."

Like rabid animals, the chained demons clamored to reach Twyla. Their growls were awful and their threats disgusting. Their teeth, malformed faces, burning skin, and wicked eyes called for her slow death.

"She's going to die a little each day," one said.

"She's already died a thousand deaths today," another said.

"How does it feel to be judged?" Apollyon said, his hand held up to maintain order. He retracted his wings and pushed her face away in disgust. "How does it feel to have things waiting to chase after you? To judge you for the way you have lived?"

She slumped, and the chains clanked. It was pointless to try to break them. It was well-known that the fire they were forged in burned deep in the center of the earth. So, instead, she kept her head down and remained quiet in her thoughts.

"It seems she doesn't like us, boys. Or maybe she's just short on words."

Apollyon's taunt only increased the intensity of threats and struggles to break free to get at her. Some of the damned threatened her with dismemberment, rape, slow and agonizing death, but mostly they communicated their hatred for her kind.

"As you can see, we don't like you very much either," Apollyon concluded.

Twyla spat at his feet, but her saliva evaporated immediately into a puff of steam.

"We had no quarrel with you, but what you've done is an act of war," she said.

"Then to war we shall go."

Twyla withdrew from the conversation with a turn of her head.

"Do you think it was something I said?" Apollyon walked away and spoke over his shoulder. "Don't worry, I have a feeling she'll be here for a long time to come. She will be broken by the time we are done with her. A mumbling mess that won't even be able to remember her own name."

The ground rumbled, and Apollyon almost fell. He staggered to the rock wall, held on, and watched the maw above slowly squeeze shut. The darkness was nothing new, and neither was the heat. But the smell of a woman . . . now that was something they all welcomed. She was a gift for everyone to enjoy, torment, and focus their rage on.

"Now that I'm free to roam about, I am going to explore the cracks beyond these shackles. See what we have access to," he said. "I'll come back to you all once I get the lay of the land. In the meantime, enjoy what I've brought here for you. I hope you'll find her to your liking. But don't wear her out too quickly. We have so much time to break her. Slowly is best, I feel. It tends to lead to insanity."

Apollyon slithered through a tight passageway and stepped down onto an outcropping of rock that gave way to a twisting tunnel that resembled a hallway. It opened up to a vast chamber, and deep down below he saw the source of heat that belched steam and toughened their flesh.

Molten earth, red with rage, splashed around and simmered.

It was so far down that the glow it gave off was nothing but a dim ray of red light. Not bright enough to reach the chamber they'd been condemned to, but bright enough for him to see minor details of the massive cavern.

He scanned the enormous chamber. Distant holes and possible passageways were all about, and he would need to explore them all. He had wondered how Asmodeus got into the chamber to make him an offer and ultimately free him from his chains. This posed an interesting problem and advantage.

Yin and yang at work again.

He might be able to get out and go topside without anyone knowing. But also, that meant they were indeed exposed to retaliation from Sariel.

Picking a fight with Death wasn't the wisest thing to do, and his only leverage against Death was chained to a wall and unable to break free.

He would have to be diligent in making sure no one got through. For his safety and that of the others. Maybe he should remain in the chamber with everyone else and collapse the rock to fill the passageway. For now, that permanent move would require some thought. No sense in rushing to a conclusion. He had some time.

In the meantime, he wanted to report back to his comrades about the lava deep below.

The other details he would keep to himself. At least for now.

CHAPTER 15

THE CABIN AND ALL THINGS BAD

After laying Cailean's body on the mattress, Sariel left the cabin by way of a secret tunnel via a trap door located underneath the table. His stiff body ached as he climbed down the rickety wooden ladder and made his way through the long tunnel filled with cobwebs, rough stone ground, and stale air. The altercation he had with Cailean and her Sins had left its mark. It had been a long time since he'd exerted such energy.

He exited the tunnel, which placed him about a quarter of a mile away from Twyla's cabin. He knew he wouldn't make it very far against Cailean's assembled Sins. There had to be thousands of them, and they were becoming more and more agitated, unruly, and unpredictable. They pounded the walls, climbed the roof, and endlessly scavenged for a way into the cabin. The old wooden planks had petrified and held against an army of aggressive beasts, but Sariel was unsure for how long. They wanted nothing more than to get at her for what she had done to them, and they didn't understand or realize that he had killed her.

The idea of them delaying him any further couldn't be a risk to take. He'd never killed a human before and was unsure what he needed to do to rid the Valley of her Sins. He was still wary of how they would react to him. He would have to think about that. But not now.

He traveled quickly, leaving the mob behind. He squeezed through the crevice in the side of the rock wall and stepped into the Akashic Halls. Sariel wasted no time moving through the hallway. His prized possessions—the books he carried—were pressed against his chest, but their pages might as well have been empty because they created a larger void in understanding, and now more than ever he needed answers.

Twyla was something more than what she'd led him to believe. Having kept a five-thousand-year-old secret was proof of that.

Sariel hurried along, pushing his old tired legs as fast as they would carry him. His dried, bloody footprints were always a map to where he had been. He retraced them to her—a reminder of deception so deep it further exposed his anger.

When he arrived at the cabin, he made sure his face was deep in the hood, his voice as neutral as possible, his presence carrying authority and fright.

"Twyla," he said, deeply and with disappointed affect. He stepped inside the cabin. What he saw sunk his mind into a lull. Feathers, both black and white, covered the floor. Furniture was broken. The fire still burned but was dim, and there was a man sitting in a chair, unmoving. The table in front of him held two amputated white wings. Immediately understanding what happened here, Sariel forgot his pain, his questions, and his anger at Twyla for her lies.

But, who was the man who waited for him? Sariel needed to be careful.

What he saw broke his heart and combined with a swift reminder that he had just killed a human with his own hands. That made him what, exactly?

"A destroyer," he whispered.

All he saw and could think about were those wings. White, stained red with splashes of blood. He didn't want to think of the pain that she went through as they were being separated from her body.

"They weren't 'separated,'" the man said.

Sariel's ire simmered. "I'm trying to minimize her suffering so it is easier for me to take," he lamented in pain.

Where the wings had been removed—or more likely where they had been torn from her body—was a moist stump of bone and muscle that dripped blood on the table. It had made its own path in the woodgrain and dripped onto the floor, where it pooled. There was a lot of blood.

Anger coursed through Sariel's veins like never before. The need for revenge blinded him. He dropped the books, circled wide, and his hands curled into fists. His mind immersed him further into murderous thoughts, and he wanted whoever this was to see his rage before he rent him.

Sariel studied the man he circled, ready to attack this strange foe at any moment. Then, a thought came flooding into his mind, and he loosened his fists. His mind detected a measure of distrust—that someone or something might be deceiving him, trying to make him believe the person sitting at the table was responsible for the chaos that had swept through the cabin.

When he got in front of the man, he found that this was a mere shell; the man inside had indeed already been killed. What sat here was nothing more than his death body. But, the dead man had been traumatized by something that worked very hard to disguise itself from Sariel. All the man did was stare straight ahead.

"Who are you?" Sariel said, knowing, of course, the answer to his question.

"I don't know," the man said. "I belong to the countless now."

Once human but now possessed by a demon. Sariel sensed it. Like he had with Cailean; Orthon thought he could hide. But Sariel always knew when they were around.

He could hear it in the tone of the man's voice, too. As he moved closer, Sariel could see what he suspected to be true. This former human was just a pawn, used by the cunning players of Hell. It had no authority and no purpose Sariel could think of. Just left behind like discarded bones at a feast. The man's tainted soul was trapped inside his body. Something held him hostage and made him do things—anything his captor desired. This man-puppet had killed. Sariel could hear the screams of his victim echoing in his head . . . He was forced to kill a friend? Sariel sensed heartbreak and regret, but it was deeply buried inside the wretch.

"I was told to be afraid of you."

"Why would you be afraid of me? I'm not the one who did this to you. I'm not the one who commanded you to kill."

"No, you didn't," the man said. "But you've done so much worse."

"Like what?"

"Death. That is what you are?"

"It is."

"You take lives. You destroy."

Sariel stiffened. They were playing with him. Using words that disturbed him.

"I think you misunderstand," Sariel said. "I give people purpose. Without death, life has no meaning."

"Life has no meaning," the man repeated. "Because death is inevitable. You, Sariel, devalue life. People fear you."

The man twitched, his mind undergoing some sort of transformation. Sariel picked up a chair and sat. He rested his elbows on the table, touched the feathers on the wing; he touched the bone, muscle, and blood. He rubbed it between his fingers and smelled it. Twyla.

He looked at the man, showed him the blood.

"What happened here?"

"Black and white had a fight."

"Who am I talking to?"

"So many more than one."

Sariel again took notice of the feathers scattered across the floor. The black belonged to a demon; the white an angel. The Angel Twyla. Somehow, he knew this was his doing. This was what Twyla was cautioning him about, but he wouldn't listen because he was so consumed with his own agenda.

"Why did they fight?"

The man sat there, stupid, unable to answer for some reason. Sariel suddenly, painfully, remembered that he had come here in anger that was directed toward Twyla.

Sariel removed his hood. His pale, sagging, old face and sad eyes almost spoke on their own.

"Look at me."

The man looked with no reaction.

"Why did they fight?"

"Black and white had a fight so he could take her into the night." He looked at Sariel, but his eyes didn't penetrate; in some way, his gaze fell short. There was confusion in there. An inner struggle raged as he continued: "But not like the night that settles here. Where she is she will be held dear."

"Where is she being held?"

"In bondage. You created the rift. The opening into what let them out. Now Twyla is left to scream and shout." The man scoffed. "You had to know they would get you back. They've been waiting, watching, hoping Cailean would take your place. Once she did, their plan went into motion only to ricochet into your face."

"What do they want to get me back for?"

"Death."

"It is my assignment."

"No, it is something more." The man gagged. "I must keep my mouth shut. It is best that way."

"Says who?"

"So many more than one."

Sariel reached across the table and took the man by the chin, Twyla's blood smearing on the man's face. Sariel focused his gaze deep into the man's eyes and saw movement behind them. Shadowed and inhuman, the insects crawled around and went about their business of rearranging things.

Sariel moved his focus inside the man's mouth. He slid his fingernails between his teeth and pried it open. Deep inside he could see the swarm nesting, infecting what was once an imperfect man, filling him with ill intent and words that were not his own.

The man bit down, his teeth gnashed, and he lashed out. Sariel pulled his hand away in time, just as the man grabbed Sariel by the throat and began to squeeze. Sariel rose to his feet. The man's strength was greater than the average human's, but it was no match for Sariel's. He peeled the man's hands away and dragged the wretch by his wrists toward the fireplace. Sariel forced him to his knees and pushed his face close to the flames.

"Who sent you?"

The man laughed. Maniacally. Without fear of the burning flames.

"This is my domain, and I command you to come out of this body!"

Sariel's robe pulled away from the heat, but he resisted the tug. He would not be deterred.

"I am in control here, demons! This is my domain, and nothing rules over me here! Nothing!"

The man trembled, flailed, and gagged. "They have her and will do terrible things to her!"

"Who?"

"Enemies, you fool!"

"I said out!"

The man heaved over and over again. Sariel slapped his back hard, and he heard ribs break. The man yelled and then laughed again.

"I'll get no answers from you. Into the flames with you all!"

"We can go into the flames with her. She'll never escape, and you'll never find her. You're going to have to live with that, knowing that we are pleased by your need to be something you could never be. You are Death. Death, Death, Death. Poor, wretched Death."

Unyielding anger tightened Sariel's face, and he pulled the man away from the fire. His flesh had been cooked by the lick of flames, and yet he still managed to laugh. Sariel pried the puppet's mouth open, slid his hand down the throat, breaking his teeth on the way in and dislocating the jaw. The man made sounds like he would be sick.

"I said to get out!"

Sariel yanked his hand out with a fistful of locusts. He tossed them into the fire, and unable to withstand Sariel's assault, the remaining locusts poured out of the man's mouth and into the flames. Sparks flew as the things sizzled and cooked, the smell terrible.

The man weakened. The skin on his cheeks had been split from the intrusion; blood covered his face. Free of possession, he fell over.

Sariel appraised him once again. He had been cleansed of the evil things, but Sariel had no time to deal with his corrupt soul.

"Unbeliever, to your feet!"

The man looked at Sariel with pleading eyes. He held his mouth closed with his own hand because it just dangled, broken.

"I said to stand!"

His mouth oozed blood and saliva. He wobbled but managed to stand.

"Get your legs about you quick," Sariel said and went to the door. "You must run and never let them catch you."

"Let oooo catt ne?" The words were mumbled and barely decipherable through the man's useless mouth. "Waat dust hattened?"

"You've died, and you are in the Valley of Death for your judgment. It is swift and precisely what you deserve. Now go."

Sariel pulled the door open. As far as the eyes could see, there were deformed creatures gathered, all focused on the man. Eager to get to him. An invisible barrier surrounded the threshold.

"Run now!"

The man looked at Sariel but hesitated. Sariel took a thunderous step toward the man and shoved him to the door.

"I said to run!"

The man tried to resist.

"No, please!"

But Sariel pushed, and the man froze at first, cradling his chin. He looked at the things all around him. Then he instinctively ran. All the monsters outside chased after him. His screams faded as he disappeared into the dense forest to forever try to outrun the creations of his sins.

Sariel slammed the door, returned to the table, and looked at the feathery wings. He picked them up, held them close to his face, breathed in the scent, and exhaled grief and anger.

"What have I done?"

CHAPTER 16

BURNING BOOKS

"Dammit!" Sariel said and slammed his fists down on the tabletop. He pounded over and over again until the thick wood splintered under the force of the blows.

His mind was a tempest of grievance and turmoil that could focus on nothing but revenge, his inner hate, and how the fire that burned within him had become an inferno.

The world would tremble.

But he had only himself to blame by baiting Cailean into taking his place. He supposed he always had his doubts that it would ever work but did it anyway to tempt fate. That left himself and his friends vulnerable.

He wished he would have listened to Twyla in spite of knowing he was destined to try to abandon his post. He had no idea his actions would condemn his beloved to God only knew what.

"You have forsaken me!" he yelled and hit the table one last time.

As if moved with the power of his mind, two books sailed across the cabin and landed in the fire. The ancient texts were the last connection Sariel had to Twyla, and somewhere deep within the coding of the writing was an answer to something much bigger than this moment. The flames licked the pages, and the old covers shrank, his opportunity burning away.

Sariel leapt to his feet, unsure how the manuscripts got there, but he needed to rescue them now. He reached his cold hand in, but his robe pulled back. He reached again anyway, not fearing the flames, and managed to nab a curled corner of the Book of Apollyon. He yanked it out and stepped on it. His bloody foot made the embers sizzle as he tried to get the other manuscript out of the flames.

But the fire had devoured it. He stood for a moment and watched his text melt away. His name ablaze like the fire within, being eaten away until it turned to char. His second profound loss in a matter of minutes.

Something told him he had lost a vital, secret message. Though he hadn't seen it before, maybe it was embossed into the pages, invisible to the eye but indented into the page to be discovered later. Perhaps he would have needed to lightly layer the page with coal to bring out the instructions. He imagined this coming from Twyla, a way of her keeping her word to him, showing her dedication and love, hoping he would find it and know what to do. But his anger had created this mess instead. On a subconscious level he didn't even want to know the message anymore; all its pursuit had brought was misery and ruin. Perhaps he had telepathically flung the books into the flames.

Clap, clap, clap.

Sariel turned around, and there was a man standing at the front door, inside the cabin. He was dressed with a touch of flair in a black top hat and pinstripe suit. He had a full, round face that seemed to squeeze his eyes shut. Red cheeks that shined in the shimmering firelight blended into a long, red and gray beard tied in a knot at the end.

"Are you done with your tantrum?" the man said.

Sariel stared, knowing a demon was in his domain—obviously a brazen one.

"Did you—"

"I didn't touch her." Asmodeus held up his hands to show they were clean. "She is someone for whom I have no concern."

Sariel pulled his hood over his head; he felt comfort, embraced the anger. He would kill this demon the way he was going to kill the being that had harmed Twyla. He would kill them all. One by one. Dismantle their army.

Invading his territory was bold, and messages needed to be sent. He would start by invading their domain.

"I didn't come here for her."

"Who do you come for then?"

The demon smiled. "Why, you, of course."

"What do you suppose to do to me? You have no authority over me!"

"No, not here I don't. I'm not a fool-hearted villain."

"What is your name, demon?"

"Asmodeus."

Sariel thought, and somehow, he knew the name. He had spoken it before but could not place it just now.

"Jogging your memory, I see. Good. Then maybe you will remember the truce we made some time ago. In exchange for you leaving my kind alone, I gave you the imps to service you and your legion of subordinates. But you failed to keep your promise when you killed a friend of mine."

"There is no loyalty among your kind."

Asmodeus laughed. "You'd be surprised by the help I had to employ to get this done."

Sariel approached, and Asmodeus grabbed the door handle. "Careful now. Don't force me to make my play yet."

"I could kill you before you knew I was on top of you."

"Maybe. Maybe not. If that is what you think, make your move." Asmodeus laughed. "Can your tired body reach me before I open this door and disappear into the night, leaving you with nothing more than the few words I have spoken?"

Sariel hesitated, knowing he could beat the portly demon to the punch but wanting to know first what his play was. "What is it you want from me then?" Sariel said.

"To see you pay for what you've done. You've killed Orthon, and that cannot be left alone. You know there must be retaliation. Don't you understand that, Death?"

"He invaded my domain!"

"You should have sent him back. Instead, you've broken our truce, forced my hand. Do you not remember that I am the Demon of Revenge? Like you, my judgment must come swiftly and at a tremendous price to the offender. That is my purpose, as yours is death. This night I have come to deliver your final punishment."

Sariel sneered, deep in the darkness, ready to chance his ability to catch this demon and teach him a lesson. "You think you can come here and threaten me? Bring me to my knees by maiming Twyla, taking her away from here?"

"Yes, in fact, I do," Asmodeus said and brushed his suit clean. He smiled at Sariel.

Sariel remained as serious as the beating Twyla took because of him.

"I really do. And I can do it because you made so many poor decisions. You've left yourself vulnerable." He pointed at Sariel. "You've done this."

"I've killed Cailean, and now my authority here has been fully restored."

"So, you're now killing the people you serve instead of sending them away or enslaving them in this hell you've created? I think you've made your move too late and made a folly in doing so. Weakening yourself just a bit more for the time being. Giving me the upper hand that I need here."

Those words bit, and Sariel wondered how true they were. His certainty of anything except his anger seemed so far away now.

"You don't stand a chance, Asmodeus. I am the lion—angry, hungry, focused—and you . . . you are the prey. I'll devour you, and I won't stop until I find where Twyla is being held. I will lay ruin to your kind."

"Make your move then, Death. Let me be the first you lay waste to."

Sariel rushed Asmodeus, his clawed, pale hands aimed at the demon's neck. He would rend him, no, toy with him; play a little before he offed him in a brutal slaying that would leave none of his kind in any doubt about the power of Death. He would deliver the body, set it at their doorstep to send a message.

Prepared for the assault, Asmodeus simply stepped aside and opened the door. A mob of deformed souls—the products of Cailean's sins—stood in wait and charged without delay.

"You see, when you opened the door to kick that man out, her Sins were lured here. Did you think the void to exact revenge for their creation would just die with Cailean? Sariel, the king of Death. The master of folly."

Sariel stood frozen, accepting what was to come. The rules of the cabins were simple: the manifestations of one's sins cannot enter the cabin that is occupied by their creator. And these sins were not Sariel's and they trampled him. They were filled with aggression at what they were, and anger that they were unable to force their maker to pay for what she had done. They knew Sariel had locked her away from them, almost as if to protect her. To them, that made him an ally—an acceptable substitute for their malice.

"Like I said, you made yourself vulnerable. And as I have suspected, you are in a weakened state. I don't know if it's emotional or physical, and I really don't care. I have simply taken advantage of it."

Kicks and punches rained down on Sariel, and the room grew full; so many things tried to get at him. They hit his head, ribs, belly, and legs. They were powerful, and they filled him with their pain—pain that could only be let out through the violence they were bred in.

"My point has been made. It was pleasure doing business with you," Asmodeus said and left.

Sariel's cloak did its best to thwart some of the blows, always serving as his protector from harm. Sariel could have dispersed them with ease, but in his misery, he didn't offer resistance because he deserved this. Every blow, name call, and pointed temper.

Stars filled his head; the thought of giving up completely crossed his mind, but he knew he couldn't even if he wanted to. He was Death, and Death could not die. Caving to his selfish whims was something he had already done—and look at what it had created.

"Wait," Sariel shouted and rose to his feet, shaking the things off effortlessly, his self-pity his biggest obstacle.

They paused, panting, fists still clenched. Sariel's blood dripped from their knuckles, splattered the floor and walls along with Twyla's.

"I can free you from this. Take you away from here. I am responsible for this and accept it. Now, allow me to right my wrong."

They remained still and looked at each other, comprehension aloof.

"If that is a sign of agreement, let us go then. Stay close. At least I can right one thing this day."

Asmodeus was gone. Sariel figured his business here was done. But Sariel wouldn't let this go. Not after what they did to Twyla. Sariel had gotten what he deserved, but Twyla . . . that was an unforgivable error within their plan. And it was time he stopped feeling sorry for himself. His heart hurt worse than any part of his body, and the only way to mend it would be to get her back.

CHAPTER 17

THE CURSED MAN

Michael Kunkle felt the heat of the day wafting off his face. The lawnmower he pushed was slowed by divots in the newly sodded lawn. Sweat dripped from his chin. His face felt like it was inches away from a furnace, and his heart pounded. He regretted buying the push mower rather than the self-propelled version. Initially, he figured it would be a great way to help him get into shape, but now he was learning it was a great way to give himself a heart attack.

"Michael," his wife, Bicca, called out to him. Her otherwise soft voice put out one heck of a shout. He heard her over the sound of the loud mower, looked over, and killed the engine.

"I've brought you some lemonade and some chips," she said. His wife was beautiful to him in every way. Supportive in his quest to find forgiveness and understanding of his father, Alister. She had encouraged him in that endeavor for years.

His father had been locked inside Sunnyside Mental Institution with the belief that Death was in love with him. The man Michael had called 'Dad' had passed away, but not before becoming something distant—someone or something else completely. That *something* his father had become consumed Michael, and he spent much time apart from Bicca and their daughter, Aimee, searching.

But he had done so much to try to make up for that.

Michael walked to the table, and Bicca studied him with care and concern.

"You need to take a break for a little while. You should sit, cool off. Your face is beet red. Maybe come in and take a cool shower. The lawn can wait until later or tomorrow."

Michael nodded. Even when she scolded him she was still beautiful.

"I don't know why you pick the hottest time of day to do that," she said.

"I never claimed to be the smartest one in the bunch," he replied with a smile.

"No," she said and kissed his head. "But the cutest one."

Michael took that compliment with a smile. He took a sip of the lemonade and made a muscle. There wasn't much there. "And with the help of these bad boys I figured I could get it done."

She winked at his lame joke, turned around, and went into the house. His eyes followed her retreating rear, and he lifted his brows appreciatively. In addition to her beauty and support, he was grateful for her sexy side too.

The glass of lemonade began to sweat as much as he did, and his mouth was already dry again. He drank some more, taking small sips, the ice cubes gently touching his lips.

His thoughts returned to his father. He often thought about what it must have been like inside his dad's mind. Having conversations with Death, believing it to be in love with him. To imagine the personal terror his father endured often gave him his own nightmares and dreams of Death. He, too, during these nightmares, thought Death was after him, and he tried to run from it. He would wake just as it reached its cold, dark, skeletal hand out and touched his shoulders.

"How are you feeling, baby?" Bicca said having returned without his notice.

Michael's reverie evaporated, and he gasped, snapping into the now.

"I'm fine," he said and raised the glass, trying to act like everything was OK. "This is delicious."

"Take it easy for a bit. Have some chips, too. You need to eat. I'll make you a sandwich. I don't want you going back out there for a while. You hear me?"

Michael nodded, and as Bicca drifted away again, his thoughts of his father came back. Dr. Lee, his father's psychologist, had gained some information from his father throughout the years, and the belief that he was cursed with Death was one of the things she had extracted. He had harped on that the most when he was lucid.

Dr. Lee believed she could cure him and worked damn hard at it. There was a moment when Michael had made a connection with his father. Not the one infected with hallucinations and dreams of the impossible. But his true father: the man who was gentle, who had taken him to the park and pushed him on the swing. The man who had thrown a football with him and showered him with affection after work. But everything went wrong when his mother passed suddenly. An aggressive form of cancer had ravaged her quickly. *Cancer*, he thought darkly—*it didn't care about age, color, or beliefs. It just killed.*

Michael reached for a chip, his eyes on the back lawn. He was more than halfway through and should be done within a half hour or so. He would wait, cool down, have his sandwich, and finish his lemonade to keep Bicca happy and off his case.

"Bicca?"

She magically appeared at the door.

"Where is Aimee?"

"She's napping."

"Oh, OK," he said, and his heart ached suddenly. He wanted to hold his daughter and never let go. That's what he wished could have been for him and his father right now, too. He'd give anything to have his father back. There was so much he wished they could do.

"You thinking about him again?"

Michael sat back. "All the time."

She massaged his shoulders. "He's in a better place."

"I know. I just miss him is all."

Michael took another chip. Bicca left a soft kiss on his wet cheek. It was soothing, the love he could feel in her gentleness.

"Well, for what it's worth, if he was anything like you, he was a great man."

Michael smiled. "Thank you."

"Now I have to go wash my face," Bicca said. "You truly are a hot mess."

Michael laughed. It was much needed. He kicked his right leg up, crossed it over his left, and sank into the seat.

"He was a great man," he said. "Really a great man who loved my mother so."

He dug his hand around the chip bowl, fished out his selection, and opened his mouth. As he tossed it inside, something hit the back of his throat.

It wasn't the chip.

The thing crawled down his throat and settled in his stomach. Sinister. Pregnant.

Michael coughed, stood up quick, and his eyes welled with tears. It was hard to suck in air. He took a drink of lemonade—at least as much as the cough reflex would allow him to—and leaned heavily against the table.

His mouth tasted funny, so he drank some more, drowning the feeling of needing to cough. Then it came over him like a wave. Severe nausea.

Sweating.

Shaking.

Worry settling in.

Bicca was behind him.

Thank God.

"Are you OK?"

Michael nodded, but it was a lie. He faced blackness. A dark wall of a tidal wave that threatened to crash down on top of him, and he did everything he could to keep it at bay.

Bicca grabbed him by his arm and led him inside. His legs were unsteady, and sweat dripped off of him worse than when he was in the heat, pushing that mower through those divots.

She seated him on the couch, felt his head with the back of her hand.

"You're burning up," she said. "Please, baby, lie down for a second." She hurried into the kitchen.

Michael did as she asked and then gagged. Then gagged again. The reflex made him sit up. The room spun, and he thought it better to listen to his wife's directions, so he lay back down.

He was scared.

Whatever this was came on suddenly and with a tremendous amount of strength and violence.

Bicca returned with a cool washcloth and placed it on his head.

"How long have you been feeling like this?"

"It just came over me," he said, his voice sore. He wanted to cough again but fought it.

"Maybe I should give you something for it? I don't know what to do."

"No," Michael said, his words awakening the itch in the back of his throat, which prompted a deep, whooping cough. "I might have heat exhaustion, that's all. I'm feeling really tired. Let me lie here for a while. If it worsens, I'll let you know."

"OK," Bicca said, her words weak and disagreeable. "I'm going to watch over you, so don't get mad at me if I keep asking how you're feeling."

"I won't."

"I think you have a fever. If it rises any more, then I'm going to give you something to bring it down and call the doctor."

Michael nodded, his eyelids like a hydraulic door programmed to close. There was strange movement in the blackness in his vision. He watched it move around for a little while. It was odd, this thing. The apparently winged thing skittered along quickly, and then would disappear, only to emerge again. It paced there, as if it were watching him from the inside.

"Heat exhaustion. I'm probably just hallucinating," he mumbled and soon tried to sleep.

CHAPTER 18

DISPOSING OF THE DEAD

Sariel picked Cailean's body up off the mattress, his arms strategically placed—one behind her back, the other behind her knees. Her broken neck made her head flop from side to side as Sariel shuffled out of the cabin.

Her Sins came to life, hitting the body, trying to rip it from Sariel's grasp, shouting and hooting wildly.

"No!" Sariel shouted. "There is nothing here for you in this shell I hold. There is no revenge! It exists no longer. Do you understand me?"

The things looked around, confused, and Sariel could only imagine how minds as damaged as these worked.

"You're hitting a lifeless piece of meat."

He turned away, carrying the body, and stepped from the thick foliage within the Valley into the flatlands where he had spent so much time. He walked, the course of his path set, the outcome certain.

"Come, stay close," Sariel said. "I don't want you to get lost in the darkness. It is easy to lose your way here. Hold onto each other if you need."

The things followed, the ones in the back pulling close to the pack, and Sariel moved onward, his pace slow but steady. This time, his footprints told a story of something he'd never done before.

He'd been doing that a lot lately—things he'd never done. He'd caused all sorts of trouble, certainly far beyond what he could comprehend. And now he had a caravan of Cailean's Sins following him.

Finally, in the distance, he could see the lamps at the bridge. Two pale specks that were a beacon of hope to so many. He never got it wrong, where to deliver the dead. But he had a failsafe, a fortunate mistake in design when he constructed this place, and that would be his saving grace this day.

He was to never kill a human. Never. He'd never even considered it, despite having witnessed the worst humanity had to offer. And yet he had done so; and he now marched across the flats with her body draped in his hands, her Sins closely behind, a despicable plan in motion. It was the only way. At least it was the only way he could conceive; his thinking had become desperate and flawed.

The lights grew closer, and the Sins of Cailean were excited by the tender glow. They swarmed like bugs to the light. Sariel let them be. It would be their last moment to celebrate before he sent them across the bridge. There were so many, and it would take some time.

"Come," he said. His large, bloody foot stepped on the first plank. It creaked something awful underneath his weight and absorbed his blood like it was thirsty. The sounds of the old bridge didn't concern the things born from Cailean's bad decisions, lies, and abuse. She was so broken, and they were so lost without her—they would follow her over a cliff.

In Cailean, Sariel had the perfect candidate, had made the perfect bargain. But it all backfired, didn't it? Who knew the full repercussions and how long they would last?

The splashing sounds of the River of Life and Death were the most soothing in the world. The peace that swept over travelers of its bridge dissolved any anger or bad thoughts and replaced them with a drive to find the other side. It was a pull of goodness.

But not for Sariel. His emotions were stuck, burning, smoldering, and they formed a lump in his chest. He needed to clean up his mess and seek his revenge—but, one thing at a time.

Sariel stopped just as the bridge sloped down toward the other side. The light was dim here . . . things were hard to see for anyone not used to the darkness as he was. This was as far as he could escort the Sins.

"Now go on," he said. "All of you. Go and be free of your suffering and constant need for revenge."

They hesitated, but one by one they walked and disappeared. A long time went by before the last one departed. The River of Life and Death awakened as Cailean's Sins were swept away and disappeared from sight. The water raged into rapids, and once Sariel could no longer see them, he approached the hump of the bridge.

He stared down into the water through the three missing slats on one half of the bridge. The hole was large enough to lure someone that should be rejected. Those who didn't belong past this point could never hope to see it, and here was where they were sent downstream. This was the first step in the process of reincarnation.

Everything would be forgotten and swept under the rug—or bridge, as it were—and thus began their chance at life anew. Perhaps a chance at a normal life. Maybe he wasn't doing such a bad thing here after all.

Sariel held Cailean over the hole.

"I'm sorry," he said, and dumped her body to be carried downstream after her Sins. His shoulders fell forward. After a moment, he straightened and felt a huge weight lifted off of his back.

"I was sent here by Twyla," Keir said.

Sariel turned around and looked at the boy in the oversized robe.

"Where did you get that?"

"I took it from Cailean. I've been doing your job, manning your post until you came back to reclaim your rightful position."

"Why did she send you?" Sariel said.

"To free Cailean. To inspire her to come after you. For you to rid deadside of your mistake. I saw what you did, and it seems her plan worked. At least the part of it that I know about."

Sariel walked off the bridge, and Keir stood near the low glow of the light. He stripped the robe off; dropped it at Sariel's feet.

"My service here has ended now," Keir said. "And that robe is never to be used again."

"Where did they take her?"

"You're asking the wrong question already, Sariel. First you need to know *why* they took her."

Sariel searched within; the answer was simple.

"They took her because of me. Because I left my post and had Cailean take my place. I killed a demon. Acted on emotion instead of making conscious decisions and taking into consideration what is right and wrong."

"Although you're correct, the answer is so much more complex than that," Keir said. "Walk me back to the cabin. This will be your last chance to rest and find some answers you've been seeking."

Sariel had no objections; only curiosity as to what knowledge the boy's mind held. He walked beside him with dead silence between them—the ironic depth of their quietude not lost on Sariel.

CHAPTER 19

ILL-FATED

Michael stood from the couch and moved to the living room, leaning on the furniture for assistance. He was burning up, disoriented. Then he heard a noise coming from the kitchen.

"Babe, is that you?" he called. "I'm not feeling well."

His body tingled. A shiny layer of sweat covered his pasty flesh, and he still had that itch in his throat and ache in his belly that felt like something was moving around in there.

"Bicca?"

She didn't respond, but the noise persisted. It sounded like something heavy being dragged.

He staggered toward the kitchen, hands sliding along the walls, his feet heavy as they scraped across the floor. He had to stop and catch his breath. His hand went to his head; the heat it exuded made him nervous.

"Hon, I think you need to take me to the hospital. Something is not right."

As he drew closer to the kitchen, he realized the noises weren't coming from that room at all, but rather, the basement.

He pressed his ear against the basement door and listened. The sound was constant, and he couldn't quite place what she was doing. The only things down there were the washing machine and dryer, which were brand new and shouldn't be making sounds like the ones he heard now.

He opened the door slowly, though the ominous creak of the door inserted enough tension to make him nervous. The continuous scratching sound grew much louder now.

"Bicca, is that you down there? What are you doing?" He paused. "Why aren't you answering me?"

He didn't get a response, but the sound remained steady and filled him with both reluctance and curiosity to see what it was.

He was unsure if he could manage walking down a flight of stairs. The banister was old, and he decided he didn't trust it.

"Are you doing laundry?"

No matter the question he asked, there was no answer. Finally, he descended the stairs, one careful, quiet step at a time. If she was working on something and simply couldn't hear him, he didn't want to scare her.

"Bicca?"

A powerful wrench in his gut bent him over, and he collapsed on the stair. He rocked back and forth, hoping it would pass soon. Sweat ran down his face, his breath stolen from his lungs as he shut his eyes and clenched his teeth.

The foreign sound came again, drawing his attention. What he heard now was more like a scraping sound.

A trowel smoothing out cement?

Something like that. Or more like an old tree limb protesting against a strong gust of wind.

He slid down the stairs on his hind end, and when he neared the bottom step, Michael came to rest and eyed the dark basement. Bicca was nowhere to be seen.

"Weird," he said and looked back up the stairs. Night had fallen, and the house was illuminated by a single lamp upstairs on the end table where he had lain when Bicca first brought him inside. His shadow was cast on the basement floor in front of him.

Maybe she was upstairs and in bed? Maybe he was here, on the bottom step, because he had a high fever and was indeed experiencing a hallucination.

"Michael?"

The sudden voice made him jump and forget about the way he felt. There, in shadow, yet not fully encased, was a man in a black robe. He stepped forward, his white hands held across his abdomen, his pinky, ring and thumb fingers interlaced, the middle and index fingers tapping together.

"I see you," the strange man said. "You have heard me, and you have come."

"Jesus!" Michael said and hurried up the stairs, testing the sturdiness of the banister and the stability of his legs. He pulled himself up as his heart pounded and his desire to get away became a mad scramble. He tripped, fell, and pushed himself back up, straining every inch of the way.

Once out of the basement, he slammed the door, rested his back against it, and tried to catch his breath. He rubbed his eyes and looked around. He felt displaced. Everything seemed distant instead of here in the now with him.

"Bicca!"

She didn't answer, and he turned to search room to room, but the thing from downstairs had somehow made it past him and stood in front of him in the hallway.

Its robe was long and ragged. The features of the face were hidden deep in the hood. It stunk of death and wheezed as it breathed.

"What—"

"Death, Michael. That is what I am. That is what you have inherited."

"No," he said and backed away from the harsh voice. "My father defeated it!"

"He succumbed to it; he didn't defeat it. There is a difference."

"What do you want with me?"

"What do you want with me?" Death countered.

"Nothing. I want to be left alone to live my life."

"You think about me often. Dream about me and call out to me. Now I have come, and you look at me like you are afraid."

"Because I am! I don't want to die! I saw what horrible things you can do to a person!"

Michael tried to see into the hood. He squinted but couldn't make out any details.

"You wish to see?"

Michael didn't answer. He was unsure what would happen if he were to see the face of death. Would it be like looking at the face of God if you were evil? Destroyed by a mere glance from Him? Death pulled back the hood enough for Michael to see, and he gasped, taken aback.

"Dad?"

"Son."

"What are you doing?"

Death pulled back his hood fully now and revealed his pale face and voided eyes. Michael took a step back. That was not his father.

"Don't fear Death. Embrace it. It can be so liberating. Besides, it is what you have now become."

"No," Michael said. "I don't accept that."

"Where is Bicca?" his father asked. "Tell me where she is!"

Michael's eyes volleyed around the room as if random household items would hold the answer.

"I don't know . . . she won't answer me."

"No, she won't, because she can't."

"Did you kill her?"

His father pulled the hood back over his head. "Oh, son. You've become sick. Infected. There is nothing I can do to help you. But I'm glad I got to see you before you slipped into a state of being unable to discern reality from fantasy. Fact from fiction. Tangled in a web of madness. It is so unpleasant, and you need to prepare yourself for it as best as you can."

"What do you mean? I am fine. I just have a stomachache. A fever, too. Besides, I've thought of *you* every day, not Death. I have to be hallucinating or something."

"This is no hallucination, Michael. It is Death you sought and Death you have found. But, unlike me, you won't run from it. You've already begun the process, embarked on a path that will change you forever."

His father turned around, opened the basement door, and entered the threshold.

"Dad?"

His father ignored him, and Michael just stood there, watching him in disbelief.

"Dad? Don't leave me!"

"Death becomes you, son."

His father pulled the door closed with a slam, and the sound jarred Michael awake. He was on the couch where Bicca had sent him to rest. The rag had fallen to the floor, and like in his dream, night had come. He had been asleep for hours.

His head had cooled, and his fever had broken. His equilibrium seemed to have returned. He sat up, groggy from sleep, but his body shook from the weakness he still felt and the details of the vivid dream. He actually felt like he was still inside of it right now.

He stood up, shuffled because his legs were heavy just like in his dream state, and his thoughts were both here and inside that dream.

"Bicca?"

He walked to the kitchen and saw his wife on the floor, blood all around her. A knife. Eyes open and accusing. A bloodbath. Words on the refrigerator, scribbled with a finger dipped in blood.

Death becomes me.

The handwriting was his. A warm sensation shot through his body as he instantly knew he didn't need to check on her. She was dead, killed by his own hands in this waking nightmare.

"Aimee!"

He hurried up the stairs as fast as he could; his daughter's bedroom door was still closed. He twisted the handle and entered the room. He didn't want to look, but he did only to immediately turn away.

"No," he said. There was so much blood. He looked at his hands. The glow of the moonlight through the curtains showed him that he was covered in crimson red.

He ran to his bedroom and gathered money, packed a small bag of necessities, and left the house in a hurry. He jumped into the car and drove away. Peering into the rearview mirror, and he could see the faint image of Death under the streetlights, watching him depart, laughing.

Michael shook. He slammed the heels of his hands into his eyes and rubbed.

"This isn't real," he said, and yet what he saw he knew to be true.

What had he done?

He immediately dismissed the idea of turning himself in. He would be institutionalized like his father. Poked, prodded, asked questions he couldn't possibly answer because he didn't understand. He couldn't sit inside a small room and wither away. He'd seen what it did to his father, and he just couldn't do it.

He pressed down on the gas pedal just a little more, destination unknown.

CHAPTER 20

RIVER'S RAGE

Cailean's body tumbled along the twists, turns, dips, and swirls of the fast-moving river. The waves picked up in intensity as her body continued to ride the rapids, headed toward an uncertain end.

The water forced her body under, slammed it against the rocky floor and into boulders, breaking her bones into bits. Her corpse bobbed up for a few moments, then dunked down again for another thrashing.

The farther she moved along the river, the more violent the trouncing became. The craggy rocks tore away chunks of flesh and mashed bone so badly that the limbs were torn off. This process continued until her entire body was smashed into tiny pieces that the water quickly dissolved as solid matter comminuted in acid.

Ahead was a spill-off. A waterfall.

The microparticles that were left of Cailean quickly reached the edge and shot out in the form of a mist, carried away by a gentle breeze.

The beautiful circular opening led to a calm, clear body of water that was home to docile fish. It was surrounded by boulders, around which unknowing people gathered in a heavy debate.

These people weren't ordinary humans, but angels who had fallen from the grace of God—and this was their version of paradise.

They had no idea the waterfall was Sariel's unique design, connecting their world to his. Or that the rapids were used to break the bodies down into a form of a mist to prepare them for reincarnation.

Unknown to the gathered group, a shrouded creature in Sariel's service remained quiet as he fulfilled his task of gathering the mist from the leaves it landed on. The design of this operation—beings to particles to mist—took Sariel years to perfect, but it had become flawless and was probably one of his greatest achievements.

Dressed in a suit of leaves and sticks–camouflage from the angels on the rocks–he used a clear jar and capped it when he was done collecting every bit of moisture that contained miniscule pulverized body parts and DNA invisible to the naked eye.

The jar was nearly full. Sariel must have sent hundreds of people over the bridge. Those who weren't meant to be on the other side or in the Valley. Bakkus had waited so long for someone to come to him and couldn't believe the jar was so full. Sariel needed him, and he was anxious to please him. While he collected the particles, there was a moment where he thought he was going to have to get a second jar. That would have been an exciting first time.

Bakkus hurried off, bent as he ran along his burrowed paths through the foliage and away from those gathered. He stopped when he reached the safety of his den, located under a large pine tree, the entryway hidden by a blanket of hanging moss and roots.

He walked into the damp candlelit room, set the jar on the table, and studied it like a prized possession. He figured he'd collected a bounty and wanted to preserve it for as long as he could. It was lonely here, and finally he had these particles to keep him company.

There were hundreds of people in the jar. Maybe tomorrow or the day after, he would make contact with some of his breeders and plant in them what had been collected. Get them back into the world.

"Maybe I'll start with Miriam, Lori, and Cassandra."

He liked those three the best. He was certain they would be excited as he. To imagine they would be giving someone another chance at life was a glorious calling. Bakkus thought pregnant women looked radiant, beautiful in what their bodies could do and glowing with the birth of life soon to come out of them.

There was a select breed that had returned to life but never grew tired or old. Their service was to re-introduce their kind back into the world. In service of Sariel and answering to Bakkus. They blended with the humans perfectly because they were human in every intelligible way. Plantings among the people.

Their fortune was that they were given another chance at life, and in turn, they'd decided to dedicate themselves to the idea of reincarnating someone in their time of need. They believed in giving others the same chance they had been given. Although it was a secreted post to be in and a controversial practice, it existed, nevertheless. A chance to circumvent the normal system of simple judgment.

Bakkus twirled the jar as he always had and found unceasing amazement at the life in there.

"Get it right this time around," he encouraged the life in the jar, which of course couldn't hear or understand him in its current form. "I'll be interested in watching how you progress through life."

CHAPTER 21

THE TALK

Sariel and Keir entered the cabin. The feathers loosed from the supernatural battle blew about in the rush of air from opening the door. Twyla's torn wing rested atop the table; the majestic white of the feathers bloomed in the twilight of the room, subtly lit up by the fireplace. Blood stained the floor, walls, and ceiling; blood that belonged to both Twyla and Apollyon. The wall was smashed in with an obvious body imprint. It told a story of great struggle and loss.

"You should know she said she wasn't going to go down without a fight," Keir said.

"You knew they were coming after her?"

"I knew when I left to go get Cailean, and before you even arrived at the halls to look for your book. I knew when you were watching me toss the water on the fire when Leo was breaking up the place. I knew long before that."

"How could you know?"

"Twyla told me and prepared me for what was to come. She told me she must do something. Make a great sacrifice to ensure you got back to where you belonged, no matter the cost to her, so that things could go back to normal. She said that I shouldn't worry. That Angelica had told her of this day. Guided her to write the books so you would know and never repeat it again."

"Angelica?"

Keir nodded.

In an explosive fit of rage, Sariel grabbed Keir and shook him. "And you said nothing to me? Why would you do that? I could have helped her. Avoided all of this. Yet you let them march her to her demise!"

"No, you couldn't have helped her," Keir said. "And I didn't let them do anything. If anyone is responsible, it is you. Now unhand me."

Sariel hesitated but let go of Keir.

"Why would I say something to you when she told me not to? I would not betray her trust as I would not betray yours."

"Because I am the ruler of this domain, and I am to know. I am to protect those who serve."

Keir just stared at him, wide eyed and timid yet resolute.

"I don't understand why! Why would you let her do that, knowing what was going to happen?"

"I asked her the same thing, resisted it, even. I told her that I was worried about her. I also explained how I felt about the things she said, but she was firm, said that it must be done. That there was no way around it and that I should do as she asked. She made me promise to keep quiet about it. I began to cry for fear of what was to come. The loss. My friend. Coworker. The woman I looked up to and served with for so long. But she hugged me, wiped away my tears, and held me close to her bosom and told me not to have a heavy heart. Instead, to have faith in the things to come. That sometimes these things were just bigger than ourselves. That we had to understand and accept these things."

Sariel hung his head and whispered, "I reject them."

"She told me that you shouldn't have a heavy heart either. She said you are hard on yourself. Confused, angry, and bitter, but so very hard on yourself. She doesn't like that. She hopes you find your way back. She said that you needed to do that. For her. For the sacrifice she gave you."

"Why didn't she tell me?"

"She said she was going to try once you took her into the Akashic Halls. I guess things didn't go the way she had planned."

Sariel wept. "She tried to talk me out of it, but I wouldn't listen. I was so consumed with myself . . ."

"I know she hinted it to you and almost told you what was about to happen. But she couldn't betray her orders. Her duty first is to serve Him. She told me this after she returned here. Her heart was heavy, and she collapsed into silence and contemplation."

"She should've told me."

"Suppose she did. Would you have listened?"

Sariel didn't answer that question because he couldn't face the answer that came to mind.

"I don't think it could have been avoided anyway," Keir said. "This, what led us here, is and was the only way. From the remnants of the battle fought here, it looks like her fear of facing the foretold past encouraged her to fight. Or maybe she had another order she hadn't shared with me. Either way, she said once it's the way it's written and placed on them shelves in there, that is the way it is going to be."

"I should look and find Cailean's book and see what it says. I had written it more than a few hundred years before she was even born. There is no possible way for me to recall what it says. I have written so many books before and since, one story blends into the other. There are just so many people . . ."

"With that in mind, you should consider returning to your post and reassigning someone to help me here. Your station has been abandoned long enough. You are needed. The real you."

"I know. I will read this book," Sariel said and dropped the burnt cover and scarred edges of the pages of the Book of Apollyon on the table.

"That book might be obsolete," Keir said. "Apollyon is the one who came and fought with Twyla and took her away. His task is finished."

"Maybe it will tell me where they took her?"

"Maybe," Keir said. "I love Twyla and want her back, too. As much as you, if not more. My hope is, in time, someone will be sent to retrieve her. It won't be you or me. She wanted to make sure that message is received loud and clear."

The thought of Twyla suffering under the hand of a demon tensed Sariel's entire body, haunted his mind. He sat heavily in the chair and smashed his fist down on the tabletop again so that, this time, the wood shattered.

"The book said I was the Fifth Angel of Apollyon. The Destroyer."

"You are indeed, Sariel. The king of the dead."

"I want to find the Book of Twyla, learn about her mission, find out where they took her."

"You can't."

"What do you mean I can't?"

"Twyla took the book, knowing that would be your next play. She sat in front of the fire, confided in me about what was happening. It was all so confusing, but her worry was not, or at least that's how she tried to portray herself as being calm and in control. She held onto the book . . . hugged it against her chest. She said she didn't want you going after her."

"What did she do?"

"She put the book in the fire. I never shouted so loudly in all my life. But she held me . . . hugged me, kissed me, and told me she did it for the love you two shared. I watched the book crumble to ash." Keir looked around at the devastation. The feathers, torn wings, the pool of blood, splatters on the walls. "Look at what has been done. I have so much work to do. I have to clean this up and try and wash away the terrible memories of what has happened here."

Sariel looked with him. With guilt came anger. The Book of Twyla had been destroyed.

Keir fed the fire some wood.

"If only I had arrived sooner . . . after discovering she had written my book."

"You came when you were supposed to, and nothing could have changed that. Not even your powers or your thoughts of hypotheticals."

"No, things could have been different. I could have arrived sooner, but Cailean had come to me, armed with information about what I did to her. She was so angry. After she attacked me and tired out, I think she wanted to walk away, submit to her Sins. I could feel it, but her fear outweighed her bravery."

"Her being there . . . that was Twyla's design, through me, of course. She did it to make sure you couldn't stop what was to happen. It was a delay tactic to allow the demons to come here."

"You know I killed Cailean because I hated what I had done to her."

"Remember what I said. Twyla wishes you to change. To try and become what you once were."

"How can I? Especially knowing what I have done? Twyla, Cailean, the demons?" Sariel felt more broken than ever. He collapsed to a knee. "I have given demons access to my domain. To harm one of my own. The one closest to me."

"That's why they went after her, Sariel. They knew that would hurt you the most. They hope you do not change. They want you to cling onto your anger, confusion, and need for revenge. To grow further and further away from the one you serve.

You need to think long and hard because this can get a lot worse."

Sariel remained still with his jaw clenched, his broken teeth crumbling. He found his fists had curled into tight balls and his fingernails dug into his palms.

"Demons have invaded my domain," Sariel said. "They've beaten and stolen my most beloved. I cannot let this go."

Keir turned away. "Then I cannot give you what I wanted."

"You keep what you have. I have no use for your toys."

"Toys aren't written in the old hand."

Sariel stood, undone, his anger palpable.

"What do you mean by that?"

"Twyla's book."

"Twyla's book? I thought you said she burnt it? Destroyed it?"

Keir nodded. "She did. But ever since I knew this day was to come, I made a copy from memory." Keir shrugged nonchalantly. "I only acted devastated when she burnt it."

"Do you have it?"

"Yes."

"Give it."

"I will not."

Sariel bent to meet the boy at his height. "I said to give it."

"I will not be responsible for causing a war."

"I will cast you out!"

"Play your hand then. You will never know its location."

"I will keep everyone from moving on. I will order every corrupt soul I move here to scour every inch of this cabin, the halls, and Valley."

"Your thinking is flawed, Sariel. You need to listen to yourself. You seek the impossible. It is in a place where you will never find it."

Sariel stood, the boy less than arm's distance away. He could grab him, force him to tell, punish him for being disobedient.

"I wrote her book, Sariel. Although I am not the original author, I wrote her book."

"What do you mean you wrote her book?"

"From memory. I told you that. I know what she's going to go through and how it will end. It is something I have tried to push deep down in the recesses of my mind. But I knew this time would come, and like you, I would have to face it. That is why I was so distraught when she told me what she must do. I already knew it to be true but was saddened that the time had finally come. I don't like it any more than you do. But we are not warriors. We serve the dead and serve the greater purpose."

"I serve my own purpose, child!"

"She wrote yours, and in a way, I suppose, I wrote hers. You wrote mine, and that is was what was commanded by Angelica."

"Take me to the book or I'll get yours."

"I can't, and neither can you. I took it. Hid it along with hers. You don't understand. She told me if you were going to go after her, she didn't want me giving you the book. She told me to watch your temper. That it was dangerous. That is why I retrieved my own book. But I, unlike you, did not read my own."

"You are sentencing her to Hell!"

"No," Keir said. "She's already there. This moment was left unwritten. Unfinished. I left it like that in hopes of your being able to change it."

Sariel's fists loosened. His anger receded at the idea of hope.

"Did you notice your book, the original one you found, was but one written page with just a few words?"

"Yes, of course."

"Because what you decide to do in this moment will write your history to come. That is my duty. I must complete the Book of Sariel by observing you."

"Let me guess."

"No need to guess, because you are right. The copy you obtained was not the original, but an effigy. I have the original, so I can write your story."

Sariel groaned deep in his throat. This conversation had reached a dead end. He would not convince the child to hand the book over to help him in his cause.

"This discussion is incomplete, and I will be back soon," Sariel said. "I have much thinking to do. I have to try and figure out what this all means."

Sariel picked up Twyla's wings and slung them over his shoulder. He took the Book of Apollyon and left the cabin. His mind was set on war. And when you go up against Death, you don't stand a chance—in that much he was confident. He owed it to Twyla, whether she wanted it or not. He would not forsake her. Keir could write Sariel's book so others could study it and fear him. Whatever else the boy might write, Death was destined to be feared. By everyone.

CHAPTER 22

MICHAEL

Michael couldn't think straight, and this was the only place he could determine to go. He pulled into the parking lot at Sunnyside Capable Care Mental Institution. He had driven around for hours, unsure of what to do, where to go. In vain he'd tried to figure out if he, too, was cursed like his father.

It sounded crazy, but the things he saw . . . the things he did . . . didn't leave much room for anything else. He didn't remember doing any of that. Was it possible to have a high fever, hallucinate, and act out a heinous crime like he had against his own family—and not remember doing it?

He hurried out of the car then ran up the steps and into the lounge area. Bonnie sat behind the reception desk, busy as usual.

"Bonnie?" he said.

"Michael!" Her surprise brought her to her feet. A wide smile quickly disappeared as she looked at him. "What's wrong?"

"I need to see Doctor Lee. Is she here?" He looked around nervously, saw movement out of the corner of his eye. His body jerked as he tried to catch a glimpse, but it moved away too quickly.

"Yes, she's here. I'll get her for you right away."

"OK," Michael said. Sweat soaked his shirt and fear enlarged his eyes.

Bonnie picked up the phone. "Please page Doctor Lee and tell her to come to the lounge. Tell her it is an emergency."

"Did you see that?" Michael said.

Bonnie looked around but said nothing.

"Look at this," he said and held up his bloody hands.

Again, Bonnie remained silent. Just then, Dr. Lee entered the lounge.

"Michael." She stopped and looked at him. "What's wrong?"

"Doctor Lee, oh, thank God. I need your help."

One who didn't know Michael would think he was tweaking on drugs.

"Slow down, Michael. What is going on? What are you feeling?"

"I killed my wife and child. I saw Death with my own eyes. I wrote on the wall in their blood that Death becomes me."

"Where are your wife and child?" Dr. Lee asked.

"They're in the house." Michael sobbed, his face in his hands. "I saw my father. He was dressed like Death. He said I have the curse, too. And I can feel it crawling around inside me. It's like an itch I can't scratch." He looked up. "What is happening to me?"

"Michael, we know there is no curse. You worked with me. You know that."

"Look," he said and showed her his blood-covered hands.

"What are you showing me?"

"They're bloody from me stabbing them. I stabbed them to death!"

"There is no blood on you, Michael."

He looked. They were covered in red. "What are you talking about?"

"Michael, I need you to give me your phone number and address so I can have the police go by the house."

"Sure," he said, wary of how she didn't see the blood. He rattled off his address and phone number, his speech fast and stuttering.

Dr. Lee nodded at Bonnie, and she picked up the phone and called Michael's house.

"What is your wife's name?"

"Bicca." Michael slapped the chair. "She didn't deserve this. She was good to me. Supported my time away from the family to visit my father every day."

"Hello, is this Bicca Kunkle?" Bonnie said, and Michael paid full attention to the side of the conversation that he could hear.

"Michael is at Sunnyside, where his father was kept. He believes he hurt you. Are you all right, Mrs. Kunkle?"

Bonnie paused.

"I see." She listened. "She sounds cute." Bonnie paused. "No, please, don't apologize. I don't mind the crying of the little one." She listened again. "No. No need for you to come here at the moment. We'll call you back as soon as we get him to calm down."

Bonnie hung up the phone and sat back down, hidden behind her computer monitor.

Dr. Lee turned to Michael. "You see, your wife is fine. You're having a hallucination. While I'd suggest a thorough work-up just to be sure, I believe this has been brought on by the stress of what you went through for so long. We should talk."

"No," Michael said. "I killed them. I saw their dead bodies. I saw the blood." He looked at his hands, and they were clean. "This doesn't make sense. I saw my father."

"No, you didn't kill them," Dr. Lee said. "And your father did not come back from the dead to haunt you. Why don't you come with me? I'll give you something to calm you down. Run a few tests when you're feeling a little better."

"Why? Why won't you believe me?"

"I believe you, Michael. I believe you think that is what happened, but you experienced a very lucid dream or a hallucination. Have you been overly stressed? Did anything happen that might have brought this on?"

"Heat exhaustion."

"Today?"

"Earlier today. Bicca put me on the couch and I fell asleep. That's when I dreamed about my father. When I awoke, that's when I saw Bicca and the baby dead." Michael sobbed the last few words.

"Come with me. Let me help you."

She took his hand, encouraged him to follow her. She led him into one of the intake rooms and closed the door.

"Lie down. Try and relax and get comfortable."

"But, the curse. Death—"

"Is far away from here, Michael. I almost beat it once, and this time I'm going to beat it. I won't let it take you."

She rolled up his sleeve and gave him a shot. The calming effects were instant. He was so tired he fell into a dreamless slumber, but his eyes continued to bounce back and forth, following the winged thing running around inside his head.

Bicca hung up the telephone and felt the cold touch of Death on her shoulder. Strange movement behind her eyes controlled her, made her inhuman, made her say and do things she had no control over. Aimee was crying, but she didn't care. Her motherly instincts had been removed.

Bicca looked at her body—or what used to be her. Knife wounds had sealed, but blood that covered the floor needed to be cleaned. The thing that crawled inside her required full obedience, no matter what manifestation it took on.

It told her Michael had been chosen first, and she was glad she wasn't in this alone. She would wait for the call and go to pick him up. Together, they would regroup and learn what was expected of them.

For now, she needed to clean up the blood and tend to Aimee. Everything must appear as normal as possible.

CHAPTER 23

FEATHERS

Sariel knelt in the flatlands, alone, ignoring those who called out to him for now. A bowl that held a thick paste and a paintbrush was set in front of him. One of Twyla's wings lay across his lap; the other was close to his side.

"I'm going to follow your advice for now. Make it seem like I've been humbled. Bide my time until I get the information I need to come and get you. I won't leave you, Twyla."

Sariel plucked the feathers from Twyla's wings, making a fluffy stack. He flexed the muscles on his own back, and his featherless wings opened for the first time in as long as he could remember. The bone frame clicked and crackled as it moved and hugged his body like a protective cage.

He wet the brush, slid it across the side of the bowl to remove excess paste, took hold of a feather, and piece by piece he began to rebuild his wings.

There was no doubt the feathers wouldn't allow him to take to flight, but he couldn't allow the beautiful feathers to remain on that bloody stump. Desecrated by a demon. They would serve him as a reminder of Twyla as he carried them around on his back. A reminder of who she was and where she was.

In Hell.

Suffering.

Because of him.

He painstakingly applied the feathers to appear as his own, paying close attention to spacing, angling, and hiding the fact that they were glued on.

When the job was finished, the feathers looked believable, and he kept the wings open, white and wide. Not as full as his once were, but full enough to look like his own, and majestic in their own right.

He took a fistful of dirt, ground it into fine dust in his hands, and covered his entire face, careful not to miss a spot. He poured the remaining liquid paste from the bowl over his own face.

He held his breath, resisted struggling, and waited for the liquid to harden. Using his fingernails as a pry, he pushed them underneath the hardened mask he had made of himself. A death mask for Death.

Sariel stood. The voices that continued to call were loud, annoying almost. He would get to them soon enough. In the meantime, he gathered the skeletal remains of Twyla's wings and walked in the opposite direction of the bridge toward the stairs that descended into the earth. He collapsed his wings enough so that they could fit into the opening of the vast underground chamber.

He stopped at the bottom of the stairs and looked at the huge hallway with stanchions in the center for support. It was long, dim, and musty. He visited often; he not only was intrigued by what was held here but also used it as a place to write the books that went into the Akashic Halls.

He placed Twyla's wings in the corner and admired his collection. Sconces on the wall burned eternal, unnecessarily lighting the long hallway. All the way in the rear of the room was a desk and chair that had a pile of unwritten books next to it.

On the left side of the room, staggered across the wall, were special death masks. Joseph Stalin, with his blown-back hair, flat facial bone structure, full mustache, and straight chin. Then Genghis Khan, with his wispy beard hanging from the mask; flat nose and wide, rounded face. Hitler, with his oval face, close-cut hair with a perfect part, and the famous mustache on his upper lip that was just as wide as his nostrils. These masks captured the essence of the evil within the men.

Attila the Hun, with his sloped forehead that ran a straight line down to his pointed nose. The long, tangled beard that would've hung down to his chest plate. Then Nero, Caligula, Kim Il Sung, Heinrich Himmler, Ayatollah Khomeini, and it continued on, disappearing into the distance. The worst humankind had to offer.

To his right hung the death masks of Jesus, Mohandas Gandhi, Buddha, Mother Teresa, Nelson Mandela, Bhagat Singh, Martin Luther King Jr., Moses, Abraham Lincoln—and like the other side, the masks faded into the distance. The best humanity had to offer.

Sariel reached into a pail and removed a rusty nail. He stepped left, pressed the nail into the hardened dirt wall, and hung his mask next to Stalin's. That's where he belonged: with the worst the world had to offer. After all, a part of him had become a part of the world, and it corrupted him.

Sariel stepped deeper into the shrine. He moved to a stanchion, and there, below the billowing flames within a sconce, sat a table with multiple artifacts. The flight log of the Enola Gay. He placed his hand on it.

"So many dead. So many for me to move on." Sariel slid his hand off the flight log. "I'll never forget that time. The evil that men do lives on and on."

A leather jacket that had belonged to a woman was folded neatly. "And you? I felt no one should know your fate. And for that I have given you eternal honor among the people. You were a woman filled with adventure and honor."

This table was one of many throughout the giant room filled with artifacts. The third item was his most newly acquired relic: a vial with blood belonging to Pope John Paul II. The fourth item on the table was a large jar filled with formaldehyde.

It was the thing within the jar that held Sariel's attention a bit longer than the other three items because this item was a mystery even to him. He wondered what information it held and why the people went out of their way . . . all the deceit, manipulation, and death for the brain of a man who had been executed. Sariel would look inside there, figure out what mysteries it held.

"I'm not in the mood to talk today, John," he said. "Maybe the next time I stop by we can chat."

"What is it you have done?"

Sariel peered into the darkness, and from deep within the cavity an Angel of Death like himself stepped out from behind a pillar. Majestic, beige-colored wings opened, and only a white loincloth covered him. He had a most-pleasant face and stood as tall as Sariel, but without the hunch.

"You've done something terrible."

"Enough to bring you into my domain, I see."

"Do you need my help?"

"No, Samael," Sariel said and turned away. "But if I did, I hope I could rely on you."

Samael smiled. Both good and evil wrapped up in one, he left the impression of giving his word with the possibility of breaking it.

"Of course you could," Samael said.

"Yes, of course," Sariel said. "Who will I get, The Destroyer or The Patron?"

Samael laughed, but not to mock. "Come, Sariel, we all have reputations in the posts we serve. Some true, others grossly exaggerated. Regardless of what is said, we serve. Do we not?"

"Hmm."

"We do as duty calls."

"Without protest, like the loyal dogs that we are," Sariel said.

"Samael is right," Samyaza, the beautiful Angel of Death said.

"Two of you?" Sariel said, the surprise in his voice impossible to hide. "Where are the other four?"

"Not coming," Samael said. "Yet. If it can be helped."

"A pity. It could've been a reunification of what has been scattered."

"For the greater good," Samyaza said.

"What have you come for, Samyaza? Have you come to observe or intervene?"

"That depends, Sariel. I'm sure you see the need as I do?"

"No, I don't."

"You've made a mask of yourself and hung it on the wall. You've put yourself on the side of evil. You're drawing attention from others."

"Yes, I know. Demons, too. I've done some terrible things," Sariel said and exited the shrine with purpose. "I have some things to make up for. Until I make up for what I have done, that is where my likeness will remain." He opened his wings fully and moved toward the voice that had been calling out to him. It was time to return to his service of the dead.

As he traveled, he would leave his wings open, allow them to dry. He thought his new appearance might bring calm to the people. It would take away from his frightening, decrepit visage. The bright white feathers instantly gave the impression of softness. Especially in such darkness.

He looked left and right at the tips of his wings and saw the feathers rippling in the breeze. In his mind, Twyla was by his side, accompanying him each and every step of the way, encouraging him onward.

With each bloody step he took, he calmly planned for war. That was the real reason why he created his own mask and placed it on the side of evil.

War with Death Incarnate was looming. For them taking his love, he would have to kill so many. One hundred times more than any bomb or plague that killed the people.

All that lay ahead was for Death and Destruction to become him—and no one would stand in his way.

AFTERWORD

After five novels revolving around a theme of Thanatology, I wrestled with the idea of joining the books together and introduce the lush world that I refer to as deadside.

The interminable task of bringing the world in which Sariel occupies was nothing short of daunting. I say this because I had five previous novels to take into consideration. Although there were breadcrumbs left along the way that the books indeed interconnect, if one wasn't paying attention to the finer details, these things may have been missed.

With that said, while writing *The Book of Sariel*, I tried to be careful tying most of the pivotal characters into my vision of what's to come. It's my hope that you found this story—the introductory to the Thanatology Series—to be of satisfaction and that my vision of the characters has remained true, kept your interest and has you excited about the endless possibilities.

www.ingramcontent.com/pod-product-compliance
Lightning Source LLC
Chambersburg PA
CBHW022044240626
47154CB00007B/2562